Fire in the Heartland

HELEN ILES

 A catalogue record for this book is available from the National Library of Australia

Published by Linellen Press
265 Boomerang Road
Oldbury, Western Australia
Website: www.linellenpress.com

DEDICATION

This book is dedicated to my great grandchildren, Caleb, Izabel, Sierra, Jakob, Timothy and Evie. May you never suffer the ravages of a bushfire in your lifetime.

It is also dedicated to all the heroic firefighters who constantly battle the fires that rage across this vast and beautiful country.

DISCLAIMER

Apart from the general location of the story,
all persons, places, names and organisations are purely fictional.

CONTENTS

ACKNOWLEDGMENTS

I would like to thank the worldwide concept of NANOWRIMO (National Novel Writers Month) for providing the challenge of writing furiously every day in the month of November. This enabled me to let the battle rage within while keeping out the critic who would stem the flow of creativity.

I also thank the Cyberette critiquing group of The Society of Women Writers WA for their comments and encouragement which kept the pen on paper to the completion of this story.

CHAPTER ONE

Rusty-spoked bike wheels hummed over the heavy layer of leaf litter, making it crackle as Clarrie took a short cut down the steep slope of Mount Beauty heading into Moreton. She would have much preferred to be riding Jasper who was steady and surefooted, not at all wobbly like this ancient contraption, but the ride on the morrow would be a hard one and she didn't want to tax his reserves in any way. As rattly as Nanna Kate's two-wheeled bike was it was still capable of weaving and ducking through the stringy-barks and saplings that had shot up on the path since her last shortcut a season ago.

She eased up on her speed a little; dropped down another rocky incline which severely rattled and shuddered both her and the bike. On another day she might have been more reckless but she could ill afford an injury that would jeopardise their plans. Already Charlie had repaired the stockyards at the back of Nanna Kate's, making them strong and unbreakable – enough at least to hold the small herd of wild horses they had come up to secure. He'd been at it for days, helped most times by Chris. Right now Chris was cleaning tack and laying it out ready for a quick assembly that evening so they could make an early start in the morning. She and Chris had been out in the hills several days ago reconnoitering the land; looking for signs of wild horse activity. Nanna Kate had even got in on the act by supplying their lunches and washing sweaty saddle rugs. Clarrie suspected however that Nanna preferred they didn't find the horses for it would be a hard and risky ride for her at sixteen, Charlie at twenty-four, and Chris, two years her junior. It would be a hard, hard ride to bring the herd home at all.

If they didn't succeed, most of those stunningly beautiful horses would be lying dead, shot off their legs from a helicopter in the soon-to-occur wild horse cull. Clarrie shuddered at the thought, and she'd seen the tear in Nanna Kate's eyes when she'd expressed that she never wanted to see that happen again. Maybe that was why she'd eventually caved to their announcement when they'd arrived in the shuddering, long, grey horse truck.

"We're going to muster the brumbies," six-year-old Shy-Lee had blurted out as she'd leapt from the running board. "All those bloody beautiful horses…"

Clarrie had clamped a hand over her mouth to stop her spilling out any more secrets. They had planned to break the news to Nanna Kate in pieces, smooth in on the intent that they would carry out the muster planned for so long by her parents. There would have been five of them on the run then, and they'd discussed their action plan of how best to bring in the herd. It would have worked a treat but now they were down to three, and the many months of planning had also been reduced, lost to grieving.

Clarrie's tears burned her eyes; she blinked quickly to stave them off; shook her head to shake away the horrific images hanging there. She tipped the bike's front wheel over the last ledge and turned onto the narrow bitumen road that wound its shaded way into town. Now she pushed the speed, firstly to clear the images tightening her jaw and burning her throat, secondly to clear the curving road that put her at great risk — each bend she rounded made her a possible victim of unsuspecting fast cars that could mow her down before they realised her presence on the road.

She pushed her thoughts to her task on this bright, stifling day and the supplies she was to procure for their ride: snack foods, cold drinks, sunscreen, insect repellent, a few coils of good stout rope to back up the well-used breaker ropes that hung on her parents' saddles, for there was one more task planned on this trip, one they hadn't dare mention to Nanna Kate – one, she hoped, even Shy-Lee knew better than to blurt out. If Nanna Kate knew she would cancel the muster: they were going to capture Flaming, the big chestnut stallion that was supposedly a direct descendent of the colt by Old Regret, a racehorse of legend who'd run loose in the high country back in the 1800s and whose bloodline had forever influenced the quality of wild horses grazing on the high plains. People had often said it was just a myth, but Clarrie's father didn't think so, and neither did her mother. The stories had been passed down to her mother by her grandfather, the renowned drover most knew just as 'Clancy', who had often tried to catch the colt.

They had never asked Nanna Kate what she really believed in case she put two and two together – and they needed Nanna Kate to be on board, for she had the land and the stockyards that backed onto the National Park, the last remnants of the old cattle way stations. From Nanna Kate's, no one would suspect the real reason for their regular rides out into the high country. Of course, they would be checking on Nanna Kate's herd of cattle, and especially on Bawldy, her hand-reared prized Hereford bull.

Around the next bend, the main street of Moreton came into view, and Clarrie felt the humidity envelope her as she whooshed along beneath the heavy canopy of giant gums and wattles. Here the air was thick and cloying, weighted by the smells of the bush. Clarrie wiped the sweat from her face and dismounted the bike; leant it up against the railing beside the general store verandah.

It felt strange seeing the mechanical contraption parked where for years she had tied her ponies, then horses, during their rides down the mountain. Even though for the past eleven years they'd lived three hundred kilometres away on 'Spur-Lea' they had always returned in the fully laden horse truck each year for the holidays, her mother never able to completely separate her life from the high plains where she'd grown up. They now farmed the lowlands, chores still heavily mingled with sideline ventures of horse breaking and training that greatly supplemented the income. That income had now become zero.

Clarrie stepped up onto the wooden verandah, her skin flushing suddenly but not from the heat. Out front of the store, on the fender of his battered green ute, sat Josh Dodson and he gazed straight at her. She averted her gaze, flicked her long fair hair back over her shoulders, annoyingly aware how ragged it must look after the wild ride down the mountain, as she'd not always been successful in ducking low branches.

She had almost entered the store when a stout figure blocked her way.

"Morning, Clarrisa," the deep voice grunted.

"Morning," she replied just as curtly, her jaw and back tightening. This was Klemm Dodson, Shire President, organiser of the wild horse cull, procurer of the helicopter pilots and sharpshooters who would slaughter all those beautiful horses from the air. The last cull had also dropped three of Nanna Kate's prime heifers – as if you couldn't tell a Hereford calf from a brumby! Hence they had also planned to bring in Nanna's herd until the cull was over as they all suspected Klemm Dodson would turn a blind eye if his shooters dropped every cow in the National Park, so intent was he of opening the park to campers and recreational resorts. Only Nanna Kate's licence to run her cattle there stopped him from doing anything more drastic, so far.

Clarrie tried to squeeze past the man's round belly but it moved into her space again. "You kids have gotta stop riding up there in those hills. The cull's happenin' soon and I don't want to see any of you get in the way of a bullet," he barked.

Clarrie's blue eyes flashed up at him and she felt her skin turn even bluer with rage. "Then stop the cull, Mr Dodson. It's cruel and unnecessary."

"Those animals ruin the high country. Ruin it! Just like those blasted cattle."

"They help it regenerate and they protect it from fires by keeping the feed down!" she bit back at him. *Heck*, she reeled, suddenly realising she'd just sounded like Nanna Kate. That's when she heard the sirens in the distance, a long way in the distance. She turned as Thomas Kellerby, the store owner, stepped out onto the verandah.

"Hey, Klemm, you gotta hear this on the radio. There's a large fire further over the mountain – they just cleared out Shingle Dale – they say they can't save the town."

Then three vehicles, red lights flashing, sped around the bend further down, each one hurtling along behind the other. Brakes squealed and squeaked as the trucks pitched and drew to a sudden halt. A young man, his face streaked with dirt, his yellow uniform similarly patterned, leapt down from the cab.

"Folks, you have to evacuate the town. There's two fires over in Glenwood that linked up an hour ago and the fire front is heading this way. It's wide and it's fast and there's no way we can stop it – it's a firestorm! You have to get everyone out of here – get them down off the mountain."

"Klemm Dodson, Shire president," Josh's dad announced, turning pale. "What do you mean you can't stop it? 'course you can stop it!"

The young fireman shook his head. "Fire front's too long. Fuel on the ground's too deep. We're going to try to hold it on the mountain but nothing is working so far. We've got to raise the alarm. You've got about three hours before it gets here. Where's your emergency centre? Your alarm system?"

By now other firefighters had leapt from the trucks. "Hey, kid," one called as Clarrie swung onto her bike, "you need to hang around so we can make sure you get down the mountain okay."

Clarrie caught a glimpse of Josh clambering into his ute as she spun the bike around and headed towards the town oval. Josh churned gravel and overtook her and she knew he would be heading straight to Grimsby Lane where his crippled mother would need help – just as she was heading to Nanna Kate's.

Her brothers and Shy-Lee were up on the mountain, sheltered from the sun and heat by thick canopies of eucalypt and salmon gums; they'd be treading over a carpet of thick dry feed from thoroughly good winter rains and sultry summer days. The whole place would burn like hell. First racing tongues of heat would swallow up the long swaying grass, then the trees, licked by dancing angels in the canopy, would explode and send fireballs out in all directions. The wooden, sun-faded walls of the homestead where Nanna had lived all her life would smoulder...

She saw these things as she pedalled, fearing how hard it would be to get Nanna to leave.

She planned as she took a different track, one that twisted and turned less steeply up the mountain, planned how to get everything out, all this on such a beautiful, clear-skied day with the sun shining brightly and a now gentle breeze blowing the sweet pungent smells of the bush all around her. How could this be happening! But now, mingled with the divine smell of the wattles and wildflowers, she could smell smoke.

❧

CHAPTER TWO

As Clarrie reached the mountain road that swept past Nanna's gate and tumbled down into the valley beyond, white fluffy clouds rose high above the trees of the ranges further north. Only they weren't clouds, she assumed. It was a bushfire.

"Fire! Fire!" she shrieked as she pedalled furiously up the drive, the bike wobbling treacherously with her efforts. "Charlie!! Chris!! Nanna!!"

Bodies appeared from various shady places.

"What is it, girl?" Nanna demanded, hobbling from the back verandah.

Nanna Kate always called her 'girl', and Clarrie suspected she no longer liked her much. And it didn't seem to matter what she did these days to make her proud nothing changed. Even getting accepted to the Equestrian College in Mansfield hadn't made her proud. She'd simply said: "There's simply nothin' there they can tell ya' that ya' good mother can't teach ya'."

But her mother wasn't there anymore, and her dreams of attending Mt Holbrook College and gaining credentials to help the family business were gone too. They just couldn't afford it – but catching Flaming would put that right again, and catching and breaking the brumbies to sell would save Spur-Lea from the Bank, for a while anyway – until they could think of something else. But now, with this fire, all that was going to be gone too.

"Charlie …!" Clarrie barked out the plan she'd formulated while riding up the mountain, "you take Nanna and Shy in the truck. Load up everything you can in the back. Nanna's precious stuff – Pebbles can go with you – she's too small to come with us; she will never keep up. Chris and I will ride the horses down into town, riding one and leading the others. You take the geese and the goats and sheep, Bess and Penelope." *That will just about fill the truck*, she reckoned.

"Chris, saddle Jasper and Monty. We'll lead Cascade, Titan and Jingo. "

"But your saddle is still in bits."

Clarrie spun. Indeed, Jasper's saddle was dismantled for cleaning; it sat alongside her mother's poly saddle, and they didn't have time to waste. "Then put my saddle in the truck and saddle me Cascade. I'll lead Jasper. And make sure you do it right – we won't have time to stop and adjust stuff riding down the hills."

Turning to check that everything living was accounted for, for nothing was ever going to burn alive if she had anything to do with it, she noticed Nanna standing fixed, her hands pressed to her pale cheeks. This farm was her world.

"Nanna, we've got to go," Clarrie said more gently, praying her matriarch would not dig in her stubborn heels to stay. There was no time to waste and already ground smoke was drifting across the hills, and the puffy white clouds were now turning black. "Come on, Nanna, we only have a few minutes. Let's gather your most precious things, just in case."

Clarrie guided Nanna Kate inside. She knew where the fireboxes were kept – all those treasured memories that were stored in a single place ready for a swift evacuation. When you live in the bush, fire was always a present danger. She helped

Nanna Kate carry the photo albums and heirlooms out to the truck, stowed them into the back seat then ran back inside and shoved a few sets of clothes into a garbage bag as Nanna Kate coaxed Baabar and Nanny up the truck ramp into the partitioned areas.

Little redheaded Shy, her long plaits in a wicked state and tears streaming down her face, brought Welsh Mountain Pebbles up into the neat miniature holding pen that was hers and tied her – not with the standard knot her siblings used but one she could manage with her little fingers.

Next, Charlie, Nanna and Clarrie herded the geese, unwilling as they were to take the long first hop up the steep ramp, but Nanna Kate bodily hoisted Goosey, the head girl, and the others rapidly followed, honking with discord as a partition was drawn across to secure them. Then Nanna Kate fetched Bessie, who stood wide-eyed, staring at the landscape, sensing that something awful was happening way out there. Clarrie then realised the wind, which had been a gentle breeze wafting to break the immense heat of the day, was now replaced by a fierce blow that dried the throat and stung the eyes.

Away in the distance, she could hear a gentle roar.

She swung Shy up into her arms and hoisted her into the back seat alongside Nanna's other precious things.

Chris was ready: her mother's enormous Cascade was saddled, her mother's standard stock whip and rope still tethered in place – it seemed wrong to take them off – Jingo and Titan were ready, tied beside each other to the railing near the drive.

"Put your seatbelt on," she told Shy. "And don't cry. Everything is going to be okay, chicken. Okay?"

"Promise?" the crying little girl squeaked.

"Promise," Clarrie smiled her reassurance, praying she hadn't just lied.

She slammed the door shut and helped Charlie secure a bellowing Bessie and winch up the ramp. "You'd better get going," she told him knowingly, "before this lot start to panic."

Charlie nodded. "Come on, Nanna, we've got to go," he urged.

But Nanna stopped halfway to the truck and turned; stared at the blackening sky beyond the national park, then at the forest beyond her back fence line. Tears welled in her eyes. "Bawldy."

Indeed, the prize of her life, her hand-reared Hereford bull, a direct descendant and last in the bloodline of the great Benwick Shady, the first Hereford imported to Australia, and the reason she had grazing rights to the high country, was still out there, somewhere.

"Bawldy?"

They each knew the fate of the Hereford herd and the brumbies if the fire indeed was unstoppable, but Charlie said regardless, "Nanna, he's smart. He'll find a way out of its way, you'll see."

Resolve washed over her, as if she needed to hear that, and slowly she turned for the truck. Clarrie sighed with relief, watched as wisps of smoke trickled above the ground around her feet. The roar had grown louder.

"You take the mountain road down, Charlie. Chris and I will shortcut it down from the last fence line and meet you on the town oval. If you get there first see if anyone has a truck that can take the horses further."

Charlie nodded then bristled, "Hell! Where is she going now?"

Nanna Kate was shuffling back towards the house. "You and Chris get going so you don't hold us up on the road. I'll handle Nanna."

So Clarrie ran for the horses. Chris had already mounted and held two of the led horses. She swung into the saddle and settled across Cascade's broad, muscular, dappled grey back. The horse jittered, its front feet lifting slightly as it spun to the sudden glow in the sky to the north and she felt the pent up power bunching beneath her. She nudged him forward as Nanna hurried back as best as her old legs would carry her, a photo frame in her hand raised up. "I've got it – we can go now," she said.

Grandpa's photo off the wall, Clarrie realised. Her life simply couldn't go on without William's stern face staring back at her each day.

Charlie helped her into the front seat then ran around and climbed in himself. He gave Clarrie a thumbs up as she untied the rope tethering her Dad's horse, Titan, to the rail, and took the rope from Chris to secure her precious Jasper.

"You go first, Charlie," Clarrie changed plans. "We'll follow you down till we hit the open bush, then we'll peel off."

Charlie gave another thumbs up in acknowledgement and started the truck, the first of the embers starting to fall kilometres ahead of the fire front as he nosed the truck into the narrow driveway.

Clarrie could feel the heat on the air, brushed the warm embers from her skin as she sent Chris ahead of her, knowing Jingo would willingly follow Monty. Bunching up, they followed the truck right out of the driveway, Clarrie seeing Shy's frightened face pressed against the glass as they drew away. She looked back. The farm had survived bushfires before 'by the luck of God' Nanna had said. With the enormous clouds starting to fill the sky, Clarrie doubted the farm would survive this time.

She heard Bessie bellowing as the truck pulled away from them.

&

CHAPTER THREE

The truck headed down the long, narrow road that wound its way into town, clearing the driveway for Clarrie and Chris to follow. Chris tugged the lead rope, urging Jingo to come alongside, electric tingles coursing through Clarrie as Cascade began to hollow his back and jog, irked by the close proximity of the two she led. The enormous silver-grey gelding that was her mother's prized possession – after all the children of course, she'd often reminded them with a smile – tossed his head repeatedly to snatch more rein. A lump rose in Clarrie's throat, and she breathed in deeply to force it back down, her gaze washing over Titan, her father's lean black thoroughbred who was as much a part of him as his children. If there was one thing that stood this family out from the rest, Clarrie realised suddenly, it was that these horses were a part of them, each and every one holding a part of their soul. "I won't let them burn, mother. I promise I won't," she murmured, pushing Cascade into a trot and sending him off down the driveway. Titan and Jasper pulled back on the ropes until they realised they were to follow, then they calmly took a position on each side of Cascade. Chris on Monty, leading Jingo, fell in behind her.

They swung out onto the roadway, the rhythmic ring of horse hooves on thin bitumen drowning out the quiet roar behind the hills and anything but shouted words from Chris. Clarrie turned in the saddle to hear his message.

"Look down there." He pointed into the distance where the main road meandered its way into Moreton. Indeed, through the trees, a long line of cars drove steadily towards town.

Ahead of them and drawing further away was the truck, Charlie driving slowly and braking frequently on the downslope. Then he pulled to the side of the road and stopped. Clarrie pushed Cascade on, wondering if Charlie was waiting for them, or maybe he wanted to talk to her.

Around the horse truck eased the nose of a fire truck. It drew alongside Charlie, and the two drivers exchanged words. Then the fire truck kept coming, followed by a second truck, drawing closer and closer. Their presence on the narrow road left no room for Clarrie and the horses, the verge blocked by high tree ferns and thick vegetation. She hated to think what was amongst it that would tangle round the horses' legs and pull them down. A short distance from her, the trucks braked and two grimy firefighters climbed down, their faces streaked with black. Clarrie drew rein, slowing Titan and Jasper, their way forward to the trail down to town blocked.

"You can't go down this way," the older firefighter said, pointing down towards the road in the distance. "You have to go back up over the mountain and go down through the National Park Road."

"But this is the shortest way to town … down through there," Clarrie argued, pointing towards the bush strip about half a kilometre away. Anger started to rise as a white haze of smoke wafted across the road further down behind the trucks, behind Charlie in the truck. He was moving again and she was glad. They didn't have any time to waste. "It's ten kilometres up and around that way."

"Can't be helped, young'un. That road down there is thick with cars and these horses will just be asking to get hit. No-one's paying much attention in their bid to get away. There's already been two accidents."

Clarrie's heart plummeted. *Ten kilometres on.* And the fire was over behind the hills. She could see doubt and worry crossing Chris's tanned features as embers landed on his tousled sandy hair. He flicked them away and swiped one off his nose.

"Besides, we have fire trucks pouring along these roads to get to a point ahead of the fire and put out any spotfires. And we need the roads kept clear so we can do that and get people out. Go on, kids. You have time to get down to town and get out that way."

Suddenly breathless, Clarrie turned Cascade back towards Chris. "We have to go back … up over the mountain road." She pointed to the winding strip behind him. Chris shook his head. He, too, knew the long ride ahead of them and wanted to get the horses off the road and into the scrub in case cars came speeding towards them.

"We don't have time to argue, Chris. Just go. Do it."

With that, Chris turned Monty, wheeled Jingo around with him, and started trotting back up towards Nanna Kate's. As Clarrie wheeled her two, Cascade lifting his feet and turning on his hind feet, the firefighter called out: "And you might need to leave those horses in town — it will be hairy enough trying to get yourselves out."

Heat burned Clarrie's nose at the mere thought of it. She shook her head. "Hurry, Chris. We've got to get over the mountain."

The loud ringing of horseshoes on bitumen echoed through the trees as they pounded along the road again, Titan and Jasper keeping stride at Cascade's hips. They passed Nanna Kate's gateway and pressed on up the hill; they rounded a curve in the road, Clarrie noting again how well the feed had grown this season; noted how it swayed and flattened in the increasing wind that pressed ahead of the fire front. This place was a tinderbox. It would go up with a mighty whoosh. "Keep going, Chris."

Ahead of the next bend, Clarrie noticed the smoke had become thicker and the smell more pungent. She drew rein, restricting Cascade's huge trot. Then flames flashed and lifted, the bush around the bend bursting into flames. Chris saw it, too, and reefed Monty around. The fire, pushed by the low, raging wind, whipped the flames across the road, blocking their path.

"We're trapped," Chris yelled back at her.

Clarrie swung around. They would have to go down towards the fire trucks. They had no choice, but a huge puff of smoke blew between them and she knew the fire was just as close that way. She scanned the fence line that separated them from town. Had it been wire she would have cut their way through, but it was posts. Big solid posts with heavy top rails. And thick bush on each side negated jumping it. Further she didn't know how far they would get before being thwarted by more solid fences. Then she noted where they were — about half a kilometre down from Benders Gully — the Overflow, a wide strip of steep, deep, rocky land that channelled excess water from the high plain basins down the mountainside. In bad winters, it tore like a torrent, making waterfalls down into Moreton and towns beyond.

"Benders Gully, Chris. We'll take them down the Overflow."

Already, she was fossicking around in her mother's saddle bag. A pair of pliers had been an essential item to carry after her mother had found a calf badly tangled in wire on a road and had no way of freeing it until Clarrie's Dad went looking for her. Her hand found the pliers and she rode up and passed them to Chris. "Cut it at one side and pull it well back so we can get through without the horses getting tangled." She reached out to take Monty and Jingo but Chris shook his head.

"You have enough to hold," he said. "I'll tie them up."

Clarrie could feel the dryness touching her throat, realised the smoke now poured around them. Red smouldering leaf and cinders started falling, the horses shaking themselves to rid it from their coats. Jasper pressed in closer to her leg and she knew he was becoming worried. Titan on the other hand, being a bolder, more experienced horse, stood taller, puffed himself and snorted. *An odd reaction to fire*, she thought. He looked ready to work, that undeniable glimmer in his eye when her Dad would ready him for cutting a cow from the herd showing how he loved the challenge. *But why now?*

Then she heard it. Felt it. A soft rumbling of the ground and a loud bawling of cattle. Through the smoke and the white gums up on the hill came more solid patches of white.

"Oh my God! Bawldy!!"

The Hereford herd lumbered down through the trees, trotting at an anxious pace towards the road.

"Chris! Look! It's Bawldy! It looks like the whole herd's here," she shouted.

"Well, let them out," he called back. "They'll be trapped if we don't, but do it now before they get too close."

Clarrie swung out of the saddle and rushed for the gate, hampered by three horses all jostling for a space on the gate's narrow opening between the bushes. The gate swung wide and inward and Clarrie stepped back amongst the horses and swung back into the saddle. Chris, his task now complete, untied Monty and swung onto his back then retrieved Jingo.

"Block the road ahead, Chris," Clarrie called. "I'll block the road this end. We'll run 'em down Benders."

She wheeled Cascade and cleared the gateway, feeling suddenly more confident in herself as he responded instantly. By now, the fluffy-headed bull was in the opening, his herd pressing forward to escape the hot wind that blew in behind them. Bawldy swung towards her and headed down the hill but only for a moment, Clarrie's waving arms, "Yah! Yah! Yah!"'s and skittering horses baulking him on his run. From beside Clarrie Titan leapt forward, keen to make his stand, as he would have done with her father on board. 'Always a natural,' she could hear her father say.

The threat was enough to turn the beast around and he turned awkwardly in the small space and sluggishly trotted uphill towards Chris. A few energetic Yah! Yahs! from Chris and he turned his head to the only option left to him – the wide opening into the Overflow. He blundered into it, followed by thirty-odd girls and a few bulky steers. Clarrie's heartbeat eased and she drew breath deeply, realised again the harsh heat that entered her lungs. They had to get moving for it was a long and rocky ride down through the hills. She hoped the way was clear all the way to Moreton.

Behind her, she could hear the sound of trucks – the firefighters coming up behind her. She heard shouted words and turned back to them. One man was standing on the running board, half in the cab and half out.

"If those cattle slow you down, young'un, you leave them behind. We'll let them know down in Moreton that you're on your way. Maybe someone will have somewhere to pen those cattle. Good luck, kids. Ride like hell 'cose that's what's coming behind you."

Clarrie nodded, and turned back to meet up with Chris; saw him waving his arms madly and pointing towards Nanna Kate's, to the gate Bawldy and his girls had just escaped through. Across the top of the pasture beyond Nanna's back fence came another menacing rumble, the thunder of hard-soled hooves.

"The brumbies!" Chris yelled. "The brumbies are coming!"

Indeed they were … and coming fast. Even through the smoke Clarrie could pick the mottle of colours – the huge browns and bays, the dappled greys like Cascade, snowy white manes and big white stripes on chestnut faces – a cream body or two with white tails streaming – some patchy duns. About forty horses in all, and there, galloping at the rear, wheeling and nipping at the round-bummed mares was a massive chestnut with four white stockings and a wide white stripe down his face. *Flaming!* He was bringing his herd to safety and she almost cried that the brumbies could be saved.

Holding back on Cascade's reins, shortening the ropes on Jasper and Titan, she sat tight as the horses streamed out onto the roadway, one after the other, some almost slipping and falling on the smooth-surfaced road, their feet so unaccustomed to it.

"You hold 'em, Chris! Don't you let them pass!"

Her heart skipped a beat as the horses picked up speed and surged up the hill, the mass of bodies pouring towards her younger brother. Behind him, flames rose, flaring with such ferocity he flinched and glanced back over his shoulder. The blaze was closer than ever.

As the horses drew near, she saw him unclip Jingo's lead rope and send the horse forward, releasing him to the herd. Fear instantly rose for Charlie's horse, for he was now loose amongst the wild ones, but they had no choice. They had to save themselves. Silently, she praised her brother's sense as he swung the empty lead rope wildly, slowing the forward rush of the brumby mob.

As the stunning chestnut stallion teetered then plunged forward through the gateway and onto the road, the quick flash of his eye alerted Clarrie to be careful on the ride. If she drew too close, she would only make that mistake once.

She brushed falling embers from Cascade's neck and sent him at a brisk trot up the hill. By the time she had joined Chris, Titan was plunging on the end of his rope, more keen to muster the herd than to abide by her strong checks to curb his dominance.

"I'll have to let him go," she told Chris as they reached the fence opening. "I can't fight him all the way down." Already, her hands felt burnt from where he'd been straining against the rope.

"Let them both go, sis. Have you ridden down here before?"

She shook her head, fearing for Jasper.

"It's full of huge boulders and fallen trees. You'll need both hands and even then we're gonna have to be careful."

As Titan half-reared in an effort to follow the brumbies, Clarrie grabbed his headstall and pulled him in close. Unclipping the rope, she let him loose. Jasper half plunged as well and she reluctantly unclipped him too. "Stay close, Jasper," she wished aloud as he leapt over some bushes and careered into the gully. Now unhampered, Clarrie had a chance to examine the route down. It was indeed rugged – rocks and boulders, standing trees and fallen trees amid a wide stretch of sloping ground secured by stout fences.

She breathed deeply, realising she'd been holding her breath each time Cascade tried to leap after Titan. "Settle. Settle," she begged him. All of a sudden the task of riding Benders Gully seemed enormous and she doubted they would make it down. So many rocks. So much debris. About two hundred metres wide of treacherous going. She wondered how many holes made by the waterfalls; how many rabbit warrens infested this place, any one able to pull a horse down and snap its leg. Her skin chilled at the thought.

"Are you coming?" Chris jibed.

She started to cough as the air thickened further with smoke. Then a wall of flames rose up behind them, and she dug her heels into Cascade's side and sent him forward – that was her only answer.

❧

CHAPTER FOUR

Down in Moreton, Charlie crawled the truck along in a long line of traffic heading for the town oval. A number of cars pulled in and parked up while others kept heading down towards the city below. Eventually, Charlie eased the truck through the chaos of vehicles and parked near where half a dozen fire trucks queued at the standpipe to reload with water. Climbing down from the cab, he asked one of the firefighters to spray water over the truck.

"It's full of animals and this smoke will kill them," he justified the request for the important resource.

"Why don't you keep going down the mountain? Things aren't going to get any better here," came the reply from the fireman manning the tanker.

"I can't. My kid brother and sister are riding down the mountain. We have to be here when they get here."

The man shook his head and looked up the steep slope where smoke billowed high into the sky and flames could be heard roaring through the trees. "You're kidding me."

Charlie shook his head, the concern in his eyes and the hard set of his jaw convincing the man he wasn't. He heard the radio crackle inside the vehicle and the man leant in to answer it.

"This is Sector Foxtrot, Andy ..." the words came clearly through the cab. "Andy, we got a couple of kids heading down the mountain on horseback. This fire is all about set to jump the road here and it'll be coming down the mountain after them."

"Shit!" the man replied, his gaze casting back over Charlie.

"Can someone get up there and cut that fence away where the gully comes out near the sale yards. They won't get out of Benders otherwise."

Immediately the man signalled two others and tasked them to open the fence at the river course this end.

"Oh yeah," Sector Foxtrot added, "they are coming down with a herd of cattle and fifty or so horses."

"Double shit!!" the man retorted, his gaze now hardening on Charlie. "What the hell are they thinking?!"

Charlie shrugged. That was just the way it was. "Do you know anyone who can transport our horses out of here when they get here?"

"Sorry, son," the man shook his head. "Most of the stock transporters have taken off already, but ask around. You might find someone still up here with a stock truck. If not, you'll just have to leave the stock behind and get yourselves out."

As the sky shadowed over them, Charlie started to walk, asking every one he passed: "Do you have a means of transporting stock out of here?"

After twenty minutes, he finally stood in the centre of the oval and bellowed: "Does anyone have a way of getting stock off this mountain. I need a horse truck urgently."

Everyone stared at him. Most shook their heads, their main concern to stick it out as long as they could, hoping the firies could put out the blaze before it reached their town, before they had to flee to save themselves.

As Charlie headed back to Nanna Kate and a teary-eyed Shy-Lee, he shook his head. What the hell were they going to do now? He couldn't sacrifice Nanna Kate's pets to take their own horses to safety – she had possibly lost everything up on the mountain … but he couldn't let all their horses die either. What the hell …? His heart thudded at the horrible choices he might have to make when Chris and Clarrie arrived if he couldn't find a truck to get them out of there.

"Excuse me. Excuse me …" A young woman in a neatly pressed shirt and tailored pants grabbed him by the arm. Charlie spun, his hopes rising. "I'm Allee … Alleena Lang, of the National News Service." Charlie noticed the cameraman panning the scene then coming to settle on him and the young woman. She seemed about his age, a bit young to be a reporter, he thought. "Did you say you need a truck? A horse truck?"

Charlie nodded. "My kid brother and sister are riding down the mountain with five of our horses. I need to get transport ready so we can get them out of here the moment they arrive." Now Charlie noticed the microphone.

"How old are your brother and sister?"

"Fourteen and sixteen," he obliged curtly.

"And they're coming down on their own?"

Charlie merely nodded, the enormity of the challenge suddenly sinking in. He gazed up at the northern sky which was further filling with billowing black clouds. "Them and about thirty cattle and fifty wild horses. And we won't have much time to get them out." He dragged his hand down the tightness of his chin, the enormity of his responsibility coming to bear. "Sorry, I gotta go and find someone with a damn big truck."

She hurried after him, her smooth, flat-heeled shoes slipping on the grass slowing her down. "So where are they coming from?”

Charlie pointed up to the long creviced crease in the mountain that was often filled with fast flowing water and a line of impressive waterfalls.

“Up there – they’re coming down the Overflow.”

The woman drew her pointed fingers across her throat, signalling the cameraman to stop filming. She kept up with Charlie as he approached group after group congregated on the oval waiting for news. “If you give me ten minutes of your time I might be able to get you some trucks,” she promised loosely. Charlie stopped and turned to her, her mode of dress alone making him doubt she would have contacts that would be of any help.

“Let me make a phone call, and I’ll get you all the support you need.”

Charlie scowled deeper.

“But I want your story, exclusive. You don’t go giving any information to anyone else but me.”

“What story?” Charlie steeled. “My brother and sister are up there with a fire roaring up their ginger and you want to find a story in it?” His resolve hardened. “How callous can people be?”

“I can help you. You just have to give me time.”

“We don’t have a lot of time,” Charlie snapped back at her.

“I know that. Now what’s your name?”

“Charlie. Charlie Darcy. My sister is Clarrisa; my brother is Chris.”

“Okay, Charlie Darcy. You watch. I’ll have a fleet of trucks up here soon.” She picked up her phone, speed dialled a number. “Hey, Boss, I have something big going down at the

Alpine Range fires," she announced, wandering slightly away from Charlie to talk. "A couple of young kids are coming down the mountain ahead of the fire-front driving wild horses and a herd of cattle ahead of them." Silence a moment, then a couple of head nods. "I need trucks to get them out once they get here. There's nothing available up here. Their brother is going to give us the exclusive in return. This is a great human interest angle of this fire – kids saving all those animals … No, the fire is still way up the mountain. I'm fine. Just a lot of smoke here at the moment. Can you get me those trucks?

"Okay. … Will do. Talk to you soon. Love you."

She flipped the phone closed and shot a look around for the cameraman. "Lew, we're going up. Dad wants some footage." She grabbed Charlie by the arm as she started walking, dragging him along with her as she headed for the helicopter parked further down the oval. "I'll need to talk to you once I get back, Charlie, so hang about and stay away from other reporters, you hear."

Charlie half nodded, his gaze turning to Nanna Kate and Shy-Lee behind the truck cab window. He would do whatever he had to do to make Chris and Clarrie safe.

The pilot, cameraman and the woman swung aboard the helicopter, the remaining crew member standing back and grasping Charlie's arm to move him out of rotor range. They stood and watched the red metal bird lift effortlessly and, nose-down, turn and glide away towards the mountain range.

CHAPTER FIVE

Up in Benders Gully, Clarrie veered around boulders and fallen trees, ensuring all the stock in the gully kept moving forward. The fire for the moment seemed less pressing, the roar distinct but strangely quieter behind them. Smoke still filled the air teasing a tickle in her throat which made her eyes water. Cascade still powered on, snorting occasionally to rid the smoke from his nostrils as he keenly sought out stock to push ahead of him. Chris rode a hundred metres ahead of her, glancing back at times to ensure she was keeping up. When the herd bottle-necked at fallen trees or extremely rocky ground, he quietly Yah-yah-ed them forward.

Ahead of her, Clarrie noticed the herd had slowed, the agitated horses now taking the lead as the cattle tired and tried to mill about to rest. "Keep them moving, Chris!" she yelled above the noise of hooves on rock and the rustle of legs through tinder dry grass. She flushed a young heifer from the bushes and sent it back to join the bulk of the herd which had now spread out across the width of the gully.

"We've got a problem," he called back to her. "Look!" He pointed to a well-treed paddock on the right, where cattle pushed up against the fence, milling about with urgency to join the rush down the mountain. He rode back to her.

"What do we do, Clarrie? There's so many of them."

She looked aghast that he should even ask. "We're not leaving them," - as if that was ever going to be an option.

"Nothing burns, Chris. Nothing burns!" she bellowed back at him.

He stared back at her, as if a sudden revelation had struck him in the face, and he heaved a resigned breath. Without another word, he dropped from the saddle, Clarrie holding Monty while he shooed the cattle back and pulled out the pliers. The cattle and horses in the gully, now not pushed so hard by the fire, broke back to a lumbering pace. Chris cut the lower wires first, snipped the top then pulled each side back to the fence posts, securing it enough to not entangle legs and horns. As he started to drop the top wooden bush rail, Clarrie's head rushed with problems she had only just realised.

"Chris, you need to get ahead of the herd again. If the cattle get to Moreton first, we won't be able to get through them to cut the fences open, so we won't make it to the oval to Charlie."

Another problem flashed. "And Charlie doesn't know we'll be coming in with this lot, Chris. What are we gonna do when we get there?"

Chris shrugged. "Charlie will think of something. He always does."

"It'll be a bit hard when he's trampled by Bawldy's mob."

For the first time since this ride started Chris smiled that devilish grin he was renowned for. "He'll deal with it."

"How's Monty holding up?"

"Fresh as a daisy and ready to run, but Bawldy's mob are tiring. He's not used to running like this."

Clarrie nodded. "While they are quiet sneak ahead of them all and get that fence open at the bottom. I'll keep moving them down." She nudged Cascade into the opening as the top rail dropped, giving Chris time to mount up and move downhill. "And don't get trampled," she said with worried affection.

When Chris was safely away, Cascade dancing sideways and back across the opening to keep old man Coskins' cattle at bay until he was, she suddenly wheeled away uphill, wheeled around again, and, waving and shouting, sent the cattle downhill after him. Cattle of varied hues of brown, brindle and grey trotted through the opening, and just kept coming. She estimated a hundred head in all. Then she heard another roar, a sound that increased the cattle's pent up fear and set the beasts leaping and jostling in the gateway. The noise set all in the gully into a nervous plunge, and sent them running again. Clarrie glanced behind her, fear suddenly rising. She hoped Chris was far enough ahead not to be knocked from his horse. He was in a very dangerous position now and she had sent him there. Her mother's words rang loudly in her ears: "Never get in front of a running herd, Clarrie. Never! You'll only ever stop the front runners – the rest will go right over you."

Then noise filled that space of thought, a strange noise not like the hiss and roar of the fire rising behind her. Ground smoke swirled up and around her. She looked up as the escaping cattle ran in a fury, more determined to clear the gateway and stay with the running herd.

Then a helicopter rose above the trees and moved slowly towards the fire. She noted, too, planes swooping low across the hills, water gushing from their bellies. The fire bombers were up.

In the National News helicopter, Alleena Lang, decked out with headphones and microphone, signalled Lewis to hone in on the scene unravelling below them, the cameraman leaning well out to get unmarred footage. He heard Allee start her commentary: "Five, four, three, two, one", and swung the camera to fill its lens with her young, intense face.

"This is Alleena Lang from the National News Service, coming live to you from the Alpine Ranges where fire is engulfing everything in its path. We have heard reports that the towns of Wakley and Shingle Dale to the north have succumbed to the flames, most buildings in the area burnt to the ground. As yet there have been no confirmed deaths but it is believe fifty people are missing in the area. The fire is heading rapidly south down the mountain with the small town of Moreton directly in its path. Roads are jammed with vehicles as families evacuate the area, leaving their homes to this horrendous, uncontrolled wildfire. The flames heading down the mountain towards Moreton are enormous, the heat is almost unbearable.

"And now, the scene we have unfolding directly below us is absolutely tragic. Firefighters reported that two young children – Clarrie Darcy, 16 years old, and her 14 year old brother Christopher Darcy – are riding down the mountain driving ahead of them a herd of fifty horses and a prized herd of Hereford cattle as they attempt to get them out of the path of the flames.

"Look down there," she tapped Lew's shoulder, instructing him to hone in further on the newly opened fence line. "We can see the herd now directly below us and more cattle are racing into the gully to join them. There must be nearly two hundred cows down there now. And there, down there, I can see the girl, Clarrie Darcy, on a big grey horse right at the back of the herd."

"Pete," she spoke directly to her news producer back at the station who undoubtedly would be watching, "these kids are about halfway down to Moreton. I can see the flames leaping up onto the ridge line behind us and smoke is starting to conceal everything. Spot fires have broken out in several places off to the side of them and these kids have to outrun whatever this fire throws at them. But this isn't their only problem — if they get to Moreton there is no way to get the stock they are driving out as all the stock trucks have already left the area and the roads are jammed with vehicles leaving. If they get this herd into Moreton there is nothing that can be done to save them once the fire reaches town."

The helicopter turned so Lew could get a long shot of the brumbies; he focused down on Chris riding at a loping canter to one side of them, then the Herefords heavy trotting a short distance behind. Then came the new herd galloping frantically to catch the front runners. As the helicopter turned again for a different angle, Cascade half reared at the giant bird circling overhead then plunged forward with a bounding stride to catch the racing mob.

Allee signalled Lew to stop filming. "Come on," she said. "We've got to get back and try to organise some trucks to get this story a sensational ending." She watched for long moments as the children below veered around boulders and kept the herd moving. This story would be her scoop of a lifetime, and she felt lucky being in the area when the fire broke out. She would milk the human aspect of the story to its end, as her father had taught her — she just had to make sure the kids didn't die in the process. Saving the herd would just be a bonus.

❧

CHAPTER SIX

Back in Moreton, Klemm Dodson thumped back and forward across the concrete floor at the Emergency Operations Centre shed, his rotund belly and arrogance getting in everyone's way.

"I can't believe you can't save this town! You've got men. We've poured a fortune of rate-payers money into this brigade to make sure it is strong and trained. Hell, they've been trained to save this town – that's what you're supposed to do, isn't it!"

Ben Winthrop stepped in front of him to stop his ranting and incessant pacing. "The men are exhausted. And what part of 'This fire is unstoppable!' don't you understand, Klemm. It's a goddamned wildfire, and this town is built totally beneath the canopy of a hundred year old growth, bush this fire is feeding on. There is no stopping it! In about an hour we are going to be pulling out of here and heading down to Boon to manage the evacuations because this fire is going to burn all the way down to the city. Right now my exhausted men are trying to hold it back long enough for everyone to get out, and rather than waste time hanging about here, you should be out there telling your people to get down off this goddamned mountain."

Dodson stood silent, his eyes scanning the maps on the wall and the long areas hatched in red. The fire front was ten kilometres long, that distance alone making the words sink in. His jaw tightening, his accusing glare blaming the Fire Chief for the failure, he suddenly turned about: "How long have we got to get everyone out?"

"Less than two hours."

Klemm Dodson turned towards the door, his wheelchair-bound wife not yet even considered. He had business papers to collect at the Shire Office before he did anything else. Then he had people to see.

As he headed for the door, a woman marking up the map asked Ben: "What are we going to do about those kids coming down the mountain. The news reports say they are halfway to Moreton."

Ben shook his head, finally realising he had a problem he hadn't yet dealt with. "Whatever we do, we can't let those cattle pour onto the oval. That's where the evacuees are holding up. It'll be disastrous. When they get here, we'll need to be ready to get those kids out of here – make them leave all the stock behind. They won't have much time before the fire is on them." He stepped over to examine the map. Finally, he said: "Okay, this is what we are going to do …"

Klemm Dodson stepped out onto the gravel skirt around the building. Yes, he definitely had people to see right now. They had to stop the livestock from getting into town.

Meanwhile, over on the town oval, Allee Lang hung on the other end of a phone call. "What do you mean you can't get trucks up here? These two kids are risking their lives to get their horses out; you can't just abandon them!"

More home truths came her way – the roads were jam-packed with vehicles, the downward route gnarled with traffic jams – the trucks simply couldn't get back up the mountain. And truckies didn't want to risk their trucks in the fire zone. Roadblocks wouldn't let them through anyway. The two truckers who had offered to help wouldn't arrive in time.

"Maybe we could find some trucks up here. Can you get us some drivers then? The kids' brother is up here with a truck load of animals so he can't drive the horses. Besides, he won't leave here until they get here. I need drivers, Pete. Find me some drivers and helicopter them in. I'll try and find trucks. Any trucks."

Down at the sale yards on the outer fringe of the city, a group of truckers stood in the undercover crib area outside the office watching news updates of the fire on a small TV. The footage of the herd surging down the gully brought silence to the banter. "Shit!" said one driver, "those poor buggers."

"Not much older than my kids," added another. "Those kids are gonna die up there, Joe. Mark my words."

On the screen, a young girl on a huge grey horse plunged forward after the streaming herd of cattle, a fast moving mixed herd that strung out along the gully and weaved in and around boulders and debris.

"Where are they taking them to?" another driver asked, picking up his keys.

"Moreton. They need to get them out from Moreton," Joe said.

"Moreton! Shit, I'd never get to Moreton in time. And there's absolutely no way to get them out of Moreton easily even if we could get up there."

"No, but I reckon we could get up to Blackfield. Look …" The youngest driver in the group strode to his truck and pulled out a road map, spread it out on the table. "… if we take Tumble Creek Road we could be at Blackfield in two hours."

"How does that look in regard to the fire?" Joe thought aloud.

Steve, the young driver, ran his finger along the line of the map. He'd been in a volunteer fire brigade with his Dad, which was sort of expected when you lived in the bush and he hadn't minded – it had given him time with his Dad and he'd learnt some life skills. Like now … he could read what the fire would do. "If the wind stays as it is, Blackfield is in the fire's path. I daresay they will be preparing to evacuate Blackfield as well. If we leave now, we could be there, set up what we need to load up ready for when the stock gets there and be gone again ahead of the fire-front."

"It won't be easy getting up the mountain roads," Stu added, not wanting to be left out of the rescue plan. "Cars are pouring out of the area."

"We'll push our way up," Joe said bluntly. 'Just hug the right lane and they'll move over. They'll know what we're going to do."

With that, five men strode determinedly towards their trucks and mounted their dusty Semis. With a roar of engines and the heavy engagement of gears, two Kenworths, two Freightliners and a Volvo started rolling.

&

CHAPTER SEVEN

Up on the mountain, Chris had worked his way to the head of the horses, thankfully protected somewhat from the dominant stallion by a group of solid mares. He spurred Monty on, intent on reaching the stretch of the Overflow that dropped away into town ahead of the herd. The gully had been fenced off after the winter cascades, effectively stopping local cyclists from scrambling their dirt bikes up the rocky climb, made more so important after one youth had been seriously injured in a fall. Chris cursed to himself that now that fence was more to their detriment than to the risk to bike riders. He wanted to hurry but knew if he put on too much speed the horses, which had now settled somewhat, having gained distance from the fire, would sense danger again and sprint to keep up with him. He gained a little more distance and glanced back. Damn! They were coming with him. He wheeled Monty suddenly, swung the lead-rope in his hand wildly above his head, and yelled and jeered the front runners, like he'd seen his Dad do at the head of a running herd. It had the right effect – the horses leading the herd suddenly propped and leapt sideways, then resisted going forward near the wild man. Their baulking caused those behind to prop and also take caution.

Chris rode on, his next check revealing he'd done well. The horses maintained a good distance behind him, which he hoped would give him time to dismount, cut the wire and get out of the way before they charged through the opening.

At the back of the sluggish Hereford herd, Clarrie kept a hold on Cascade who wanted to get in amongst them and hurry them along. She could feel the power of him, his muscles bunching; he could become quite a handful if too frustrated, and she remembered at times her mother had chastised him for bullying the steers. How she wished her mother was riding him now as she tried to hold him back, knowing how strongly he wanted to be with Titan who was running somewhere up ahead of the cattle. She now had two hundred odd beasts strung out between her and Chris and worried how he was fairing in the lead. She glanced behind her, checking the bright red sky and the blackness of billowing clouds. The whole world behind her was ablaze. Intense heat swirled around her, leaving her breathless. Her eyes watered as the smoke dug in, clogging her airways and stinging her eyes. Embers that had fallen on her skin left black streaks where she had swiped them off, and tiny holes had appeared in her shirt. They'd been riding about an hour, therefore, they had to be at least halfway to town.

She worried then – if Chris opened the fence to town, would Charlie be ready? Would he even know they had this many running in the herd? Had it been just Bawldy and his girls, she and Chris would manage to keep them contained, but an extra hundred cows and fifty wild horses, they had no chance. If they made it through the lower opening, they could spill out all over town and run into traffic. They could greatly hold up the people trying to escape town. She shook her head as Cascade started dancing on his toes again and she sent him on after the herd, praying again that Chris was okay because she just could not see him.

Further, she had to be extremely careful for up ahead trees that had sprung up amongst the rocks and had managed to hold fast throughout the winter deluge threw out thick low branches.

She could not afford to be knocked from Cascade, and nor could Chris from Monty.

Occasionally, up ahead, she could see the stallion's chestnut head rise up out of the pack as if he was checking on the safety and whereabouts of his mares. She prayed he stayed safe himself and that he did not see Chris as a threat and attack.

For now, though, the rhythmic thunder of hooves drowned out the roar of the fire and the crackle of dry grass at their feet. In an hour, they would be in Moreton and could rest the tiring herd. *Be ready, Charlie. Please be ready.*

Inside the Emergency Operations Centre, Ben Winthrop added more red lines to the map. The fire front now stretched across the top of the ridgeline, but a wind shift due in an hour would fan the flames directly downhill again – south, where everyone was heading. And the fire would speed up again.

"How long do you think it will take to get here," Sue Chambers asked. She had kids at home; she needed to get to them and get them out of Moreton.

"About an hour. Once it hits this area," Ben pointed slightly to one side of Benders Gully, about where Clarrie and Chris had released the cattle, "it will get into that huge belt of gums and start throwing fireballs out all over the place. That's when we kiss Moreton goodbye. Is everything packed up here ready to go?"

Sue nodded. "Everything is in your car – you just have to take the radio and maps."

"Well, you better get going, Sue. Get yourself and your kids out of here, and drive carefully. Everyone's in a panic, and the smoke is providing little visibility."

She nodded again and headed to the door.

"Ben …"; he looked across at her. "… what about those kids up on the Overflow? Do you think they'll make it?"

"It'll all depend on when the wind changes," he said solemnly. But it put his mind back to the dilemma he still had to consider. He'd been told the fence to the Overflow had been cut away, which it needed to be to get the kids out of there, but that would also release a considerable number of livestock into the town, in amongst the fire trucks on the oval and the townsfolk not yet ready to join the long queue of vehicles crawling down the mountain. Then the cattle would mingle with the traffic. One accident anywhere on the road and a hundred or so people would be held up on the road waiting for it to clear as the fire-front raged on through. Alone in the Operations Room, he now had time to think.

He picked up the radio. "Does anyone know if those sharpshooters who were here for the cull are still in town?"

Across town on the oval, Allee Lang went in search of Charlie. She'd found and chatted to Nanna Kate and Charlie's young sister, who were both watering the animals inside the truck to keep the animals in comfort. This story, she realised, was even bigger than she'd thought. At twenty-four, Charlie was head of the family, their parents having died in a horrific car accident six months earlier. Between Clarrie and Charlie, they were trying to make ends meet, trying to keep the family together. The family farm, the estate left to them all, was still indebted to the bank and the bank wanted to foreclose, doubting the children could keep up the repayments.

"This is their last ditch effort," Nanna Kate had said. "They came up here to rescue the horses from the blasted cull and intended to truck them home for breaking and selling. That would get them out of a bind for a while, maybe, and save the horses from future culls. Now this, and they're going to lose everything. Poor little blighters."

To Allee, that made it even more sad. To lose your parents and then your home. And to make things worse, the fire was against them. She'd just heard from Pete that they couldn't get any trucks up the mountain in time. There was absolutely no way to get the stock out.

She found Charlie standing on the upper rim of the oval, staring up at the mountain. He didn't look at her when she arrived beside him and she noticed a tear line down his cheek. He heaved a deep breath. "I can't get any trucks to get them out," he said. "I've tried everything – asked everyone. They're going to get here expecting me to have something ready to load the horses onto and there's nothing. And I've gotta get Nanna and Shy out of here before the fire gets here. What if they're not here by then? What do I do?"

"Oh, Charlie." Moisture glimmered in Allee's eyes too. She'd said she'd get trucks. Just give me your story and everything will be okay, she'd said. She shook her head. "I wonder how far up they are." She couldn't tell him she couldn't get trucks either, but guessed her silence would have told him that. She placed a hand on his shoulder. "You need to save Nanna and Shy-Lee."

More silent tears rolled down Charlie's cheek and she realised he must have already known that and accepted it. She turned and strode back down the slope to find Lew. They could go up and check out the fire again, hover over the gully and at least be able to tell Charlie how far away they were; maybe how long it would take to get there. Then he would know how long he should wait.

Her phone rang, which surprised her. Signals had become intermittent with the smoke layers blanketing everything. She kept the caller on the phone.

"Charlie! Charlie!!"

He turned with reluctance.

"Where is Blackfield?"

"About two hours down the mountain, that way," he said glumly.

"Charlie! We've got trucks! We've got trucks, Charlie!!"

More tears flowed down his face and he dragged his hands down his cheeks to wipe them away. This was the miracle he had obviously been praying for.

"But they can only get to Blackfield. Can Clarrie get the herds to Blackfield?"

Charlie, now re-enthused, strode down the slope towards her. "The Overflow runs all the way down – that's where the floodways cross the roads." He pointed to a barren area at the far side of the oval where the land flattened then dipped away again towards a dry river bed. "It's fenced at the roads in some places, like here, but it will take them all the way to Blackfield."

"Yes!" Allee fisted the air beside her face. "Yes, they can get to Blackfield!" she shouted back into the phone. "We'll see you in Blackfield."

"But there's a problem," Charlie added, pointing up at the top of the slope where the cattle would come pouring down onto the oval. "There's two hundred metres of open ground between the end of this stretch and the next secured stretch of Benders. There's no way to keep control of the line to force them down onto the next stretch. Once they break through there they will be all over town. Clarrie was going to meet us here at the oval to truck the horses out. That's where she'll be heading."

"Things have changed a lot since she left the top of the mountain, Charlie."

Alleena half walked, half ran across to the stand pipe where three fire trucks were filling their tanks with water. She chatted to them for a moment then waited impatiently as one of the men climbed into the cab and picked up the radio. He climbed down a moment later and gave her a nod. Then she jogged back to Charlie, a grin spreading across her face.

"It's sorted, Charlie. Lew and I will go up and see where Clarrie and Chris are. I'll see you shortly."

As she headed across to the news helicopter at the far end of the oval, Charlie watched as the firefighters rallied those standing around near vehicles and cold barbecue pits. A few moments later, cars started up and began manoeuvring into position, the first row lining up one behind the other on the far side of the barren stretch. Fire trucks and more vehicles parked parallel to them but eighty metres away. Two more firefighters cut away the wire at the next rocky descent on Benders Gully, ready for the herd's arrival. A radio call telling the Controller that all was in place completed the task.

The helicopter lifted off and, nose down, headed away up the mountain, Charlie watching Allee attach her headset as the aircraft thudda-thudda-thudda-ed away.

Once airborne, Allee Lang drew Lew's attention to her; signalled him to turn on the camera. "Five, four, three, two, one. ... Yes, this is Alleena Lang reporting from the Alpine Range fires that are currently bearing down on the small mountain town of Moreton. We've been told the fire will reach

Moreton within the hour and you can see the stream of cars escaping from the area in an effort to be well out of its reach.

"In the distance, you can see the extent of the fire-front. It is absolutely huge. It is ravaging the national park which will take years to recover from its intensity. We can feel the heat from the fires even up here."

The helicopter swung around and directed its nose south; the pilot pointed animatedly down.

"And down there, below us," Allee announced, a lump forming in her throat at the horrible realisation that tragedy was so close to happening, "are the two young riders driving a large herd of cattle and horses down the mountain to safety. We can see from here the fire is only a kilometre or so behind them, but smaller fires are springing up amongst the trees off to their left and right. They just seem to start with a puff of smoke then bam! It flares and there's a new fire spreading closer to them than the main fire-front. These recently orphaned kids are risking their lives to save these animals and must now drive them further down the mountain to the town of Blackfield. We believe a convoy of trucks is pressing its way up the mountain road to Blackfield to assist with transporting the herds out of the area. We've also been told Moreton is under evacuation orders and the town will be impacted by fire within the hour. We can only pray these kids get through town and on down the mountain before the fire gets there. We will keep you posted with further reports as they come to hand.

"This is Alleena Lang for the National News Service."

Allee felt the sting of smoke in her eyes and wondered how the kids were coping closer to the ground. Indeed, a heavy pall was now starting to block out vision as the smoke from closer fires penetrated the trees. She picked up the loud hailer and asked the pilot to fly lower. "I need to get a message to those kids," she explained.

Below her, Clarrie coughed violently as the smoke billowed up from the ground, the downdraft of the helicopter also sending up sand and grass stalks into her face. She shielded her eyes and wished the damn thing would go away. Each time it came near Cascade became more difficult, and now at this low height it was causing him to panic and undoubtedly blew dirt into his eyes too. She had him running at a steady trot now, the tired Herefords looking for spaces to hunker into and stop. Bawldy was closest to her and she worried that the stress of the run would be too much for him. He was the heaviest beast in the herd and not overly fit after grazing on the abundant feed in the Park. The helicopter set him to running again and she looked back and up and waved it away. Lord knows things were hard enough as it was without it causing more harm. She heard a voice shouting down from the aircraft.

"Clarrie Darcy ... Clarrie Darcy ... if you can hear me, give me a signal."

She heard it plain and clear; gave a thumbs up, a signal she and Charlie would often use when running stock on opposite sides, just ensuring all was safe and good.

"Clarrie, you must take the herd through Moreton and on down to Blackfield. You can't stop in Moreton. Do you understand?"

She gave another thumbs up without losing a stride from Cascade; she had to keep up with Bawldy. But the news concerned her. Blackfield was hours away; she was so tired; the Herefords were lumbering and wanting to stop; she could only imagine how stressed the cattle and horses up ahead were feeling. Moreton was about their limit of endurance.

The voice came again. "We can't get trucks to Moreton to get you out – you have to keep going."

She nodded then gave another thumbs up. That's why they had to keep going. They would get to Moreton ahead of the fire but then the fire would catch them. She drew rein sharply, holding Cascade tight for a moment to get her message across.

"Tell Chris up front," she yelled back, pointing to the front of the herd. "Tell Chris." There was no way she would get to the front to warn him and Chris expected to open the wire fence and drive the herd onto the oval. There was no other plan.

"Okay. Good luck!"

With that the helicopter lifted and Clarrie was pleased. The higher height had less effect on the herd. She readied herself in case it lowered again to alert Chris, who was now about a kilometre ahead of her, the herd that strung out. A low flying aircraft ahead of the herd could bring it to a halt or, worse still, stampede it back in her direction. She had to be ready. She had to be ready to turn it back again if that happened. Sending Cascade forward again, she fumbled with the leather thonging that secured her mother's stock whip to the saddle. They each knew how to crack a whip; her Dad had taught her and practiced with her since she was a toddler, her whips growing in length in direct proportion to her height as she grew. In the Darcy clan though, only Charlie, her Mum and Dad were allowed to draw their whips when running cattle – she and Chris were considered too young yet to know the exact moment it would have the right effect. *Too Gung-ho*, Charlie had often ridiculed them in their younger days. But here she was now, her mother's stock whip in her hand, still coiled as it had been when tethered to the saddle. She could ill afford the length of the lash to tangle Cascade's legs or snag on a bush and tear it from her hand.

She leant further forward and peered through the smoke to see if the herd remained moving forward. "Yah, Bawldy. Yah!! Yah!" She set the generous red backside back to shuffling southward.

In the helicopter, after the message had been passed to Chris from a height, Allee said: "Let's fly on towards Blackfield, see if we can get some footage of those trucks coming up the mountain."

&

CHAPTER EIGHT

Back on the oval in Moreton, Charlie stood on the truck's front fender, watching the opening to Benders Gully. Smoke had been wafting into town for the past hour, getting thicker and thicker, and poor Shy-Lee's eyes had been watering almost non-stop since it had started. Nanna Kate now sat with her in the truck, a moist towel covering them to reduce their redness. She had said very little since their escape from her farm; she was probably silently grieving, Charlie realised. She'd been as hard hit as they had this year, losing a daughter and now the home she'd lived in all her life. That National Park, or most of it, had at one point belonged to her family until the government reclaimed it in the name of 'conservation'. Only because the family had imported the first Hereford herds into the country, cattle that had grazed the high plains since their arrival, and because Bawldy was the last stud bull from the original bloodline, was Nanna Kate permitted to maintain a small herd of Herefords on the national park. For the past decade, however, she'd been plagued by the local Council to relinquish her rights to the land. But that would mean getting rid of Bawldy and his girls, for she just did not have enough land left to maintain them.

Charlie turned slightly, wondering what she would do now; wondering what they would all do now. Only two days ago he'd argued with Karl Bradley, the Bank Manager, and while they were staying at Nanna Kate's there was not much he could do to resolve the matter the man was concerned about. They just needed more time, he'd told him. If Clarrie and Chris could get this herd down to Blackfield, if they could somehow manage to get them back to Spur-Lea, all they needed was time to handle and break a few. If Flaming was with the herd they could start their own stud farm, keeping a few of the best mares to breed from. But first they had to get them through to Blackfield.

Overhead he could hear the gentle thudda-thudda-thudda of the helicopter returning. It had been gone a while; in fact, he'd thought it had returned earlier as another helicopter had flown in and landed further over behind the Council building. He noticed the Fire Chief pull up and survey the barrier of cars lined up on both sides of where Benders Gully would normally channel the overflow from the mountain down through town, cascading it under the bridge to wend its way down to other National Parks closer to the city, filling many water catchments on the way. The section of fenced gully started again on the far side of the bridge.

Behind Charlie, Alleena Lang and the cameraman hurried towards him; Allee scrambled up onto the front of the truck beside him. "Hey, Charlie."

"Hey," he replied.

"They're doing okay up there. They should be here soon. We've just been down to see how the stock trucks are doing. They're having a hard time getting through – the road is jammed with cars trying to get down. The Police are down there now trying to get everything moving and we did a report about the urgency in getting these trucks to Blackfield to pick up the herd. It looks like they were trying to get a Police car in front of them to escort them in."

She stopped talking as the Fire Chief called out through his loud hailer. "Listen up. Listen up, everyone! Everyone, stay between your cars. As soon as this herd moves through to the bridge, we are going to start moving you down the mountain. Please keep going till you reach the city limits. Nowhere on this mountain is a safe haven right now. Please keep going to the city. Anyone who does not have a means of getting out please come and see me. We will be moving out as soon as the herd passes through. Be ready to wave your arms and keep the herd in between the vehicles. Frighten them back if they try to escape. Please be patient. It won't be long now."

Charlie then noticed a few men walking across from the Council Office, each carrying a rifle. Klemm Dodson shuffled after them, his round belly rolling around him as he tried to keep up while shouting instructions. The men climbed onto the front of the fire trucks and took a position with a good view of the Overflow, prepared themselves for shooting.

"What the ….?" Charlie leapt down from the fender and hurried across the raceway. But the Fire Chief met him halfway. "What the hell are you doing ..?"

Allee checked that Lew was filming. Every piece of footage they could gather was going to make this a truly explosive story. The trucks pushing their way through erring traffic had brought a lump to her throat. She didn't know who these men were, but she was sure going to find out and add them to the story. Hell, this was the stuff movies were made of. And now, here was Charlie taking on armed shooters, taking on the authorities controlling this incident.

"They are only there to drop anything that tries to get over the barrier," the Fire Chief shouted above the din of anxious people and the wind that swept down the hill. "We simply cannot have anything running loose in the traffic as we try to get this lot down to safety. It's in everyone's best interest."

"It's not in my brother and sister's best interest. They are in amongst the herd. What if they get in the way of a bullet?"

"These are sharpshooters, kid. They know what they are doing?"

"I don't care. It's not worth the risk."

But his words were drowned out as a woman screamed, and half the crowd gasped. In the sky beyond the trees red clouds billowed skyward, the fire suddenly raging up, then black filled the sky like night had suddenly fallen. One of the shooters slid across the bonnet of a car and jogged across the open ground; took a position on the front of another car, aimed ready. Charlie could feel the vibrations of the ground beneath his feet, like an earth tremor, but he knew it for what it was. The herd was coming! He hurried back to the truck, heard a shouted order come from the other barrier.

"You drop that bull!"

The words turned him cold. He knew it was Klemm Dodson, and he knew exactly what he meant. Diverting his course, he climbed up alongside the sharpshooter, unassumingly ready to block his shot if he had to. He wondered how many others had been given the same order. Bawldy was the target regardless what he did and Charlie could only block one barrel.

Loud crackling filled the air, teasing the hair on the back of his neck, and the ground shook harder. Then, from out of the smoke, shapes appeared.

"Get this, Lew!" Allee urged. "Follow their run down the gully!" But Lew was already primed, the camera on his shoulder already gathering footage to fly back to the station.

Horses appeared, just a mass of heads at first, each stretching and receding as they bolted through the opening, the front runners immediately baulking, skittering, spooking sideways then back again, unsure of which way to run – all these odd shapes and the smell of humans panicked them more than the fire behind them, almost sending them spinning on their hind legs back the way they had come. But embers fell around them, pinpricks of red stinging their skin, melting their coats. The sky behind them flared again, blew ferocious and hot. Two brown haltered horses barged through the pack and bolted to the front and just kept going, noticeably searching for an opening to flee through. Chestnuts surged up beside them, focusing on the clear open space under the bridge ahead. They rushed onward, horse after horse pouring with them. White ones, brown ones, gold and cream ones, ones with white patches, ones with black manes and tails streaming, all thundering through, then a solid dark chestnut, the colour of fresh liver, a wide white stripe breaking the dark in two as it trailed down his face. The long white stockings stood out in Lew's camera lens as he powered by kicking up clods of dirt, a stunning creature to even to the most inexperienced eye.

One after another, they coursed through, then bunches blurred his screen. He could feel the truck bonnet vibrating from the power of their feet. Then they were gone, and there in front of his lens was a boy, maybe not much older than his own kid, streaked with dirt and wide-eyed, a handkerchief tied around his head to cover his mouth. He was there one moment then gone again, cheers from the crowd urging him on as he flattened down along his horse's neck to miss the bridge beams and all Lew could see for a matter of seconds was a bouncing bottom in denim.

He swung the camera back again as cows gushed from the opening, running hard and stirring up a heap of dust in their awkward, unbalanced gait. He coughed, not sure if from the smoke or the debris being kicked up from the ground. Cattle streamed across his screen like a dark shadow, mostly dark shapes glistening with sweat. Some bellowed, but most just chased the horses. And they just kept coming. A few of the stragglers slowed and eyed the barriers, started heading that way and Lew shuddered at what he expected to happen next; he hoped they were diligent back at the station and edited this out if it suddenly turned ugly. One sharpshooter rose to his feet to get a better shot, but people rose from behind their bonnets and began waving their arms and shouting, turning the cattle back into the raceway. The cattle pounded on, bee-lined for the bridge, following their faster brothers.

Then silence. A long moment of nothing. Charlie's heart hit his stomach. Where was Clarrie? She was well back from Chris. Too far. Was she even still part of the ride? Cascade could be quite a handful at times and had there been more time he would have helped her rebuild her saddle so she could ride Jasper. And where were the Herefords? He leapt down from the truck. Would he have time to go up and find her?

As he reached the gully opening, the ground started to shake again. Something was coming and he swung back out of the way, climbed up on the front of a car. He didn't know whose, and he didn't care. But here was better than standing where he was.

Out of the smoke came patches of white, those always white faces even in the dirtiest weather – then chestnut bodies, roly-poly trotting, heavy-footed girls regally making their way down the raceway, like models on a catwalk, implying nothing much bothered them. In the distance, he could just hear words:

"Yah! Yah-Yah!!"

A lump stuck in his throat. It was Clarrie. He counted cows – fifteen – twenty – all strung out the length of the raceway, in ones and twos like ladies on a city stroll. Twenty five. Thirty. And Bawldy, lagging tiredly behind. "Yah! Yah! Yah!!" came Clarrie pushing him along. Charlie glanced back – the sharpshooter on his side had risen to his feet.

"Guard Bawldy," he shouted at Clarrie, the desperation in his voice obvious as Clarrie scanned the cars. All the worry she'd had of losing the herd in Moreton poured out of her, this town holding back leaving to help them save the stock. People cheered as she trotted into the raceway, but all she could see was the few men on the truck bonnets with their rifles aimed at Bawldy. Immediately she knew what Charlie meant and her skin turned cold.

Sitting deep in the saddle, she rapped Cascade's sides with her heels and in three giant bounds she was beside the gentle beast, shielding him, staying with him, ready to shoulder him over if she had to. Her eyes widened as rifle barrels followed her, followed Bawldy from the other side. She couldn't cover both sides. And at this speed he was an easy target.

"Yah! Bawldy. Yah!" She had to get him out of there.

Up ahead she could see Nanna Kate, the old woman leaning out the window of the truck, waving her arm towards the bridge. "Go on, Bawldy, you old bastard; get yourself outta here! Look after your girls!"

Clarrie noted Nanna Kate never said a word to her, reminding her that Nanna Kate didn't like her much. She'd pretty much stopped talking to her since she'd pushed her parents to let her go to Equestrian School, and especially since the car accident. Had her parents not gone out that night to discuss what was involved in her taking up those studies, they would never have been on that road at that time – never been at that intersection at that precise moment when the truck had barrelled through. It was all her fault …

Her thoughts elsewhere she was caught off guard when Cascade suddenly plunged forward then bounded on the spot, his head thrashing violently as he tried to shake the reins from her hands. The cavort almost dislodged her; yanked her forward as he snatched the bit to run. She rose in the stirrups to strengthen her leg hold, to stop getting jolted from the saddle. Her eyes fixed on the shooters now across to her left, their aim unhampered; their aim true. More cheering went up and grew suddenly louder. Then a face appeared on the other side of Bawldy's, a face staring straight at her, smiling. It was Josh Dodson.

"Where'd you come from?" she shouted, awed.

"Jumped in over the cars. Come on, we've got to get Bawldy out of here. We've got to keep him between us."

Tears welled in Clarrie's eyes and a lump blocked her throat. "Thank you," she squeaked as her eyes burned with moisture.

"It's okay. My Dad's an arsehole. Come on, let's get Bawldy under the bridge."

As they bypassed the shooters, Clarrie took a rear position to guard Bawldy's behind, then sent him on with a light rap of the folded stock whip, sent him running on to catch the others.

When they'd both ducked beneath the low beams of the bridge and disappeared, Lew shut down the camera.

"Did you get it? Did you get it all?" Allee wailed with excitement.

"My oath I got it all," he grinned.

"Okay, well, we'd better get out of here. Our pilot's looking rather distressed."

Right then horns started tooting and the line of cars started moving methodically down onto the road.

ॐ

CHAPTER NINE

Once under the bridge they rode in thicker country, the flatter ground more like a dry river bed than a gully. Bawldy shuffled along trying to find less rocky ground and Clarrie realised his feet must be bruised from the swift pace she'd maintained over the sharp rocky descent further back. White sweat had broken out on his coat and she wondered how long he could keep going.

"You really should rest him a while," Josh said. "He's looking done in. And it's not helping any of them heaving in all this smoke."

"But the fire …"

Josh nodded and glanced at the sky behind them. "We'll make better time in the long run if we slow them down for ten to fifteen minutes and let them catch their breath then they will be ready to run again if we need to. You reckon?" he nodded again.

Clarrie nodded, sought out the distance between her and the front of the herd. "Chris will still be running them."

"I'll go get him and bring him back – it's a long ride into Blackfield and the herd can't get off the gully till Chesterley Road."

Clarrie frowned but Josh was riding away.

"Josh," she called out after him, "what are you doing here? You should be with your Mum?"

"She's out and safe. I came back for Jesse." He patted his little bay stock horse's neck, wheeled her and, standing on his stirrups, overtook Bawldy and his gaggle of girls and sprinted down the gully after Chris.

Left alone, Cascade started to sweat. He was brilliant at working stock, especially in the company of others, but alone his boldness seemed to falter – it seemed all the huff and puff was to convince himself of his bravado when really he found safety in numbers. She now knew what it had been like for her mother, her legs straddling the broad back and sides, feeling all that bunched up power, waiting for him to cavort and veer, the arching of his massive neck as he bunched even further, knotting up his muscles in readiness for its unwanted release. When it came it would be humungous. She hoped she could hold him together until Josh and Chris came back for if he took control of the reins now he would bypass Bawldy and the girls and possibly send them back in the other direction.

So she sat, feeling Cascade's energised bounce plop the saddle against her seat; she kept her feet jammed down flat, not giving him heel to go, nor toe down submission. She just sat, calm, cooling her thoughts and fears with breath; realising how hot the air was in her throat, how pungent the humidity. She sucked in the smells of the bush and the sweaty cows ahead of her; the smell of sweat on Cascade's neck and the smoke pooling around their feet. The smoke made her want to run again, especially with it being so low. Smoke hung mostly above the ground and if she dismounted and led her horse she would breathe much easier, but in this fire, the smoke was everywhere, at every height, the only thing different was the thickness. She wondered if Nanna's house was still standing. And what would she do if it wasn't? She played with the reins, moving the bit softly in Cascade's mouth, slightly left, a little right, holding then vibrating left again. *Too much – don't turn his head. Right rein. Breathe.* She felt the monster horse settle beneath her, realised the soft movement of her mother's hands on the reins was what made him putty beneath her.

"Settle, boy, settle," she soothed, a tear rising to her eye as she heard her mother's voice in her head.

Oh what's to become of us, she murmured inwardly. *Why can't you foresee what's going to happen during the day so you know not to get out of bed; so you know not to do the things that will get you killed.* Anguish gripped her chest. She fought it back. The feeling was not new to her, only the times it appeared was different. She fought the image of the truck – a big blue semi – polished chrome over the grill – big solid 'roo bar. Speed. Brakes screeching. The 'roo bar round her window. The car barrelling sideways, the acrid smell of tyres; black smoke, screeching. The car spinning. Pain as her head hit the window. Glass exploding. The car airborne. No, she was airborne. She shook her head, winning over not wanting to see any more. Not wanting to acknowledge the heat billowing around her.

Cascade suddenly propped, and nickered. She caught her breath as Josh and Chris trotted up towards her. Behind them the Herefords snatched at grass and plodded quietly on, like they did when she rode out with her Mum and Dad to move them to more abundant pasture on the high plains. Of course they would eventually go seeking better feed themselves, but Nanna Kate liked them to be moved before an area was stripped beyond repair. She knew her cattle management, that old lady, and certainly should have coming from the Clancy clan, the high country Clancy's at that. Her grandfather had brought the Herefords to the mountain pastures in the late 1800s she'd been told, her mother proud of their cattle-king, drover heritage. But she'd been even prouder of their equestrian feats for which they were renowned.

"The herd has slowed," Chris said, looking rather tired and somewhat battered. His shirt sleeve was torn, and a trickle of blood aborted rolling down his cheek. "I hit a tree branch," he said, noticing her interest. Then his face brightened. "Did you see Flaming, Clarrie? Flaming's with the herd."

"Where's Titan and Jasper?"

"Jasper's running with the herd and staying out of Flaming's way …" Chris grinned. "Titan is keeping Coskins' cattle together and pushing them where he wants them to go – he's having the time of his life."

Clarrie eased up on Cascade's rein now the horses were back. Her hands felt raw from fighting him. She turned and looked at the world behind them. "It's like Armageddon," she said, remembering reading something about the end of the world.

"The Apocalypse," Chris added.

"Judgment Day … Da, da, da, dah," Josh threw in his contribution.

"How long do you think it will take to get here," Chris asked him.

"About two hours, maybe," Josh said, "so we'd better get moving. We've got some problems up ahead that we'll need to plan for."

"So you know Benders …" Clarrie assumed, feeling relieved. She was glad Josh had come back for Jesse; she thought better of him now, knowing his horse meant that much to him. But she should have expected it, she realised, given that he was always kind to the mare when they'd come across each other up on the high plains. She'd never seen him yank her in the mouth, or boot her in the ribs, and if she tripped and her mouth was jabbed by the bit, he would apologise as if it was his fault. Maybe that was why she liked him so much, even though she'd tried to hate him because Klemm Dodson was his Dad. And you can't trust a Dodson. That's what Nanna Kate always said.

Josh's lips twisted and he half-heartedly shrugged. "I was one of the town louts that caused the gully to be fenced. You know … one of those crazy moments when you have a bike and think you're invincible. Broke my leg in two places. Me mate broke his back and Benders was deemed dangerous rather than us being stupid." He shrugged again. It was not worth worrying about now – too late after the event.

He clapped a couple of times, sending Bawldy forward again. He didn't mind 'slow' but 'stop' was not acceptable.

❦

CHAPTER TEN

"We've got about an hour before we get to Chesterley Road. They've put swinging gates on both sides of the road but the gully widens and the fence to the gate is only a top rail so the cattle can bolt straight underneath. The horses won't like it though so we have to get those gates open before the herd gets there. Then we've got to hold them so they make it through and across the road to the other gateway."

"What do you mean 'hold them?'" Clarrie watched Josh's face. She'd been watching him so long over the years she'd been coming to Moreton she could read his real meaning like a book. This expression was one of worry – deep to the point of desperate.

"Chesterly Road is three k's long – the gully and floodway are about the halfway point. If one cow or horse breaks off down the road either way we could lose the whole lot. They've put up road blocks at both ends of the road but only barriers to stop cars taking a wrong turn down the mountain – they won't stop cattle. So we've got to get every cow and every horse across the road and in through the other gateway."

Clarrie heaved a breath. This ride was getting beyond a joke.

"There's another mountain road about half an hour from Blackfield – same deal with that. We just have to hope the fire is far enough back at each crossing so we can do it slow and calm and without giving them a need to scatter. Then we can run them on into Blackfield."

"And that's another problem," Chris voiced his own worries. "Once in Blackfield where do we put them?"

"And we have to find Charlie," Clarrie added.

"The showgrounds. We'll run them to the showgrounds. It's close to the Overflow and well fenced once we get them in there."

"Then what? Do you think the fire will reach Blackfield?"

"This fire isn't going to stop for anything," Josh huffed, shaking his head. "But I heard on the radio earlier trucks are pushing their way back up the mountain against the flow of traffic to get to Blackfield to pick up all the stock. We just gotta get them there."

For the first time since riding to town that morning, Clarrie smiled. And Josh smiled back at her.

"We'll keep moving them along for a while then Chris and I will go down ahead of them, open the gates and try to stop them getting loose on the road. You just keep driving them forward."

He shrugged again as if that was the only option they had. And it was.

Right then a loud booming whoosh filled the air, and the ground shook. Every single beast in the herd leapt forward and Clarrie, Josh and Chris spun to see three huge fireballs explode into the air.

"Shit! That's got to be gas tanks blowing up in Moreton." Then another enormous ball of flame vented skyward, swirling and imploding in reds, golds, and black. "And that's gotta be the gas station. We'd better get outta here before the Supply Yard goes up – if they didn't get them out already, there's thirty-odd gas cylinders sitting there ready to blow."

As another explosion rent the air, Josh, Chris and Clarrie leapt forward and incited Bawldy and his slow girls to get moving. The rest of the herd had already plunged forward and were surging away from them … fast.

Down in Blackfield, Charlie parked the truck in the coolish shade of a tree grove, as much for the animals in the back as for Nanna Kate and Shy-Lee who were both looking distressed. He borrowed a fire hose and showered water all over the cab and horse box, the pouring water slightly cooling the air around it and diminishing smoke. He refilled water buckets and pushed them inside, accepted a couple of bottles of water from a generous firefighter – an old man to be fighting fires, Charlie thought. But then, if he didn't do it, who would?

"Take care of yours, young'un," the man said, making sure the bottles were cold. "Lots of prayers going on out there for your brother and sister." He swung around as fireballs shot into the sky way up the mountain. "And they'll be prayin' for 'em a lot harder now."

"Charlie Darcy! … Charlie Darcy! … Charlie, where are you?"

Charlie recognised Alleena's voice. "Over here." He waved his arm high from side to side.

The reporter with the long blonde hair had now tied it back in a neat ponytail. She looked a lot younger than she had earlier, he thought. Probably in her early twenties. But he must have been wrong purely for the position she held on the News Station.

"Charlie, we need to talk. I need a lot more information … this story has gone global and the Station's been flooded with calls. My Dad has got hook ups going all over the place. I need more background to feed the public."

"To milk this for what it's worth, you mean. Christ, lady, my kid brother and sister are up there. And that's where I should be, looking after them. Maybe I should be pulling them in and leaving the herd behind … just to get them out of there. Look, the whole mountain is going up!" His hand went to his forehead, panic growing as fireballs ripped into the sky. "Jesus! What am I going to do? – I can't lose them too."

"Charlie! … Charlie, listen to me. Lew and I will go up shortly and see where they are … get some footage so the public stay on side with this. You have no idea how the public can help you. Right now you've got to think about what you need to do here for when they arrive."

Charlie looked blank-faced.

"What is going to happen when the herd gets here, Charlie? What are your plans?"

He shook his head; he'd not even thought about it. Originally they'd planned to capture the herd and take them to Spur-Lea a truckload at a time. Clarrie had it all planned out. She had the vision of how they would survive – all he had to do was keep the Bank Manager away and bide them some time. But he bet her plans hadn't expected fifty horses to be up on the high plains – they expected ten or twelve at the most. And he'd never considered Bawldy's herd. He'd just never thought. He shook his head again.

"We've got trucks coming, Charlie. The fire's still coming down the mountain and we've got trucks coming up to get the horses and cattle out. That's as much as I can do. You have to tell me what else you need to be able to load them, and we won't have much time to do it. I've just heard the wind change they were hoping for to blow the fire back up the mountain isn't expected for another hour or so. Blackfield is directly in the path of the fire."

Charlie's face paled. "Those horses and cattle won't be able to run any further than this. We can't expect them to."

"Then find a solution, Charlie. Start with … where are you going to put them when they get here and how are you going to get them there? We'll talk when I get back." She swung up onto the truck, leant in the window and put her hand on Nanna Kate's arm.

"How are you doing, Nanna?" she asked, knowing the woman had lost her whole world up there on the mountain. She'd heard quite a bit just standing around listening to people, especially about the Council plans for the high country and how the old lady had been treated.

The old lady looked up at her with watery eyes. "I'm fine, dear. And Shy here is fine too. We just want to get Bawldy and his girls down off the mountain, don't we, little one?"

A teary-eyed little girl screwed up her face and nodded.

"It won't be long now," Allee told them.

Jumping back down, she headed across to Lew, signalled it was time to go up and see where the kids were.

"Just a quick jaunt," he added. "This chopper needs to get back to the city before the smoke gets too thick and too much ash gets in the air. I noticed the other chopper left a few minutes ago."

Allee climbed into the back seat, giving Lew prime place again to film regardless of the aircraft's direction. She put on her headphones. "I want to scoot down the hill a bit first," she said, "… check out where the trucks are." He nodded and the pilot lifted the bird off the ground and swung away to the east.

Below them the mountain was aglow with every colour imaginable for fire. Reds, golds, yellow tongues, brown, black and grey. Trees higher up the mountain looked like candles with just their tips ablaze. And flames still poured down the mountain like lava, consuming everything in its path.

Down on the mountain pass the traffic was flowing, hundreds of cars thankfully doing the right thing as Police directed them over. And up the steep mountain pass came the five heavy Semis, each pulling a double line of trailers. They were chugging up slowly, but they were coming.

Tapping Lew on the shoulder, she started her commentary, becoming more confident now in front of the camera and for a brief moment she hoped her father would be proud of her. He had placed his trust in her when no-one else was able to take the flight up Roper Mountain for what they thought was a minor fire outside of Lake Jewels. My god how wrong they were.

"… you can see down below the trucks making their way up the mountain pass towards Blackfield. We can only hope all the livestock will fit onto those five trucks. And we pray they will arrive in Blackfield in time to load up and get back down the mountain to safety. I heard a short while ago Blackfield is now preparing for evacuation, the push down the mountain due to start in about ten minutes."

"The smoke is incredibly thick up here now, but we are going to attempt to fly over to where Clarrie and Chris Darcy are bringing the horses down along this place called the Overflow. In winter, this is apparently a truly spectacular place where water courses tumble and turn into waterfalls that feed the rivers all the way down to the Forrest National Park just outside the city. It is a totally different scene up there now and these kids just have to get down through that dry river bed into Blackfield. We should be coming up on the herd very soon."

❧

CHAPTER ELEVEN

After a few minutes of running, the herd settled again and maintained a steady trot over flatter ground, scrambled more over rocks and sharp stones. The tree canopy mottled and darkened the ground as thick white clouds blotted out the sun. Clarrie noted Josh was right. Bawldy and his girls looked much fresher for the long minutes of easy walking.

She realised shortly after though that they had started milling about ahead, that the front of the herd had stopped moving forward. Chris and Josh had ridden off to get ahead of the herd and settle it before they reached the gateway, but she noticed Josh pushing his horse back through the mob, squeezing Jesse through narrow spaces and tapping bovine backs to make them move aside.

"We've got another herd up ahead," he shouted to her above the noise of hooves on rocks and the crackle, roar and hiss of the fire behind them. "We've got to keep the herd moving past them."

"No! You have to let them out!"

"No, Clarrisa! We won't be able to manage any more stock than we have. They'll have to stay."

"No! You tell Chris to let them out! They'll be trapped where they are. At least if we let them out, they have a chance to outrun the fire." Her scathing expression struck him like a brick. "You let them out, Josh Dodson, or I'll hate you forever. You let them out, or I will!"

Josh heaved a deep sigh, caught the billowing smoke pouring into the sky behind them. They just didn't have time to argue. Without another word, he turned and pushed his way back down to the front of the herd to direct Chris and open up the corner section of the paddock fence.

Another hundred cows scrambled through the opening and joined the ambling herd, with much lowing and panic in the increasing heat.

Josh and Chris swung back on to their horses and eased back to let them pass and infiltrate fully with the herd.

"They'll need time to sort themselves out," Josh said as Clarrie arrived at the break in the fence, his obvious frustration making Clarrie feel guilty. "…and we need to be ready for when we open those gates and cross the road," he added before she could defend herself. He went on to tell them they had to guard each side of the road and be ready to drive them back if they tried to break away. "Pull your stock whip ready, Chris. You might need it if the cattle try to get past you, and I have no idea how they will react now this new mob is in the bunch. But no snap cracking," he added, "just a light flick of the lash in front of their face to warn them back. With them this nervous, any loud retorts and we'll panic them all over the mountainside."

Ah, so this was what her folks had been concerned with when laying the rules about who could and could not use the whip on a muster. She and Chris had always been too exuberant when sending the lash out.

"You just keep 'em coming slow," he told Clarrie as he tipped over a steep descent. "The longer it takes them to cross the road, the more control we'll have over them," his voice muffled amongst the rocks between them. "Are we ready?" he asked, appearing out from behind another boulder.

Then he and Chris loped off to ease up the pace and swing the gates wide. They were soon swallowed by the smoke, leaving Clarrie alone again, alone to feel the heat of the day on her back and the heavy smoke burning her throat, nose and eyes; alone to wish Charlie was here with her … to wish her parents were with her. Charlie would have enjoyed this ride much more than she. Not that she didn't like driving stock — it's just that she liked driving stock on Jasper, with Charlie on Jingo over on her right and her Mum on Cascade over to her left. Chris would be further up the line, steering the lead with her Dad. Titan loved taking control — *the control freak.*

She heaved a deep sigh, knowing those days would never come again, and it was all because of her selfish wish. Nanna Kate was right — her mother could have taught her everything she needed to know about horses and jumping and competing, but no, she had to go to Equestrian School. She wanted to be like all those toffy-nosed girls in their posh white jodphurs jumping over pretty coloured fences. She wanted to ride in the shows and represent her country; she wanted to be good enough to ride in the Olympics. Inwardly, she shook her head. No, she didn't. She shook her head physically. She just wanted to show those stuck-up toffs that she could outride in her scuffed-up moleskins and battered Williams boots. She wanted to show them you didn't need lessons to jump a four-foot fallen tree trunk on a downhill run or shoulder a bull around to get him in the pen. You didn't need lessons for that — you just watched your Mum and Dad and did it. But oh, how she wanted that Equestrian School Certificate to hang on their wall at Spur-Lea. That Certificate would make such a difference to other folk. It would help the family business if one of them had some sort of school credentials with horses. She could have helped her Mum with the fineries of horse schooling and show education.

Something plopped down alongside her, almost hitting her leg, and her attention idly followed it to the ground. By the time it landed, Cascade was already past it, and she looked back, and noticed more leaf litter dropping around her. Where it touched down, smoke started rising, then flames. Small at first, but soon they puffed themselves to a tongue that waved in the wind, spread out to greet other flames. A line of trickling fire sprang across the grass behind her, like someone had laid a petrol line and ignited it.

"Shit!!" she squealed. It wouldn't take long for it to flare once it hit the trees. And it didn't take long to flare as a helicopter rose above the trees, the down draught fanning the flames and feeding them. Damn, she was going to have a go at that News station when she got a hold of them. "Yah! Cascade, Yah. Yah, Bawldy. Get them old legs moving," she screamed. She cracked the whip, pulling back at the last second to avoid a snap-cracking retort. She just wanted Bawldy to pick up the pace then the girls to pick up theirs. "Fire! Fire! Get moving, Chris!!"

She hoped he could hear her; she hoped he would be well out of the way when the cattle started to run.

Then she heard a loud retort, and just in front of Bawldy the ground kicked up some dirt. For a moment she thought Chris had snapped the stock whip, but the sound was too close. Not echoed. Bawldy spooked sideways as she realised the retort had come from beside her. She looked up. The helicopter was there, and she realised the man leaning out of it didn't have a camera. It was a sharpshooter, a culler.

The helicopter turned, and flew over her as Bawldy stumbled into mottled ground beneath the trees, the shooter's new line seeking him out through the branches. Cascade had already picked up speed from the turbulence overhead and she reined him in hard against the low tree branches, ducking to avoid hitting her head. The move blocked Bawldy's run back into daylight. Cascade's shoulder pinned the bull against the tree trunk and Clarrie could see the shooter's dilemma through the withering branches; he wanted to take the shot but she was in the way. Behind her, flames rose higher and started eating the ground towards her. The heat intensified, the glow of the flames burning her face. *Oh my God, what do I do?* she squealed to herself. *What do I do?*

She knew if she released Bawldy, the man would shoot him down. If she didn't, they would both be burnt alive. "Go away!" she screamed at the helicopter. "Go … away!" She waved her arm across the space in the branches, further blocking his shot, but the move relinquished her hold on Cascade, giving him leeway to back away from the tree. Bawldy started to move, but she went with him, half her attention on Bawldy's line, the other on the rifle aimed at this precious bull. Pitched down on Cascade's neck, she ran him clear of the trees, staying stride for stride with Bawldy's run – if the helicopter changed sides, she would pull back and guard him from the left. She could do that across the clearing, but it would be more difficult to do amongst the trees.

Ahead of her, the Hereford girls had also started running, the thunder of their feet spurring Coskins' cattle to run. The helicopter swung over to the other side, inciting the flames to flare and leap back on that side. Clarrie checked Cascade with a sharp tug and brought him round to Bawldy's other side. She stayed upright and moving about in the saddle to further detract the shooter's aim. He wouldn't dare fire with her so close to his line.

Then the aircraft rose up, swirling smoke and ash and embers everywhere; it hovered almost over her head. She couldn't possibly get in the way if they fired from over the top of him. "No!" she screamed. "No!! Bawldy, run!!"

Down at Chesterley Road, Chris and Josh dismounted and swung the first gate wide open to the road. Dragging Monty after him, Chris hurried across and opened the second gate, struggling to fully push it into the gully so the stock wouldn't get hung up on it.

Josh let his stock whip trail out along the bitumen. "Get yours ready," he said. "If Clarrie brings them along nice and steady, we might be able to push them on through."

"You reckon?" Chris huffed doubtfully. The width of the road and verges was more than generous, more than he would be able to cover if the herd tried to break past him.

"If she brings them calmly, maybe. How's she doing by the way?"

Chris looked up the gully where the shade and smoke mingled, where the canopy of trees darkened everything further. "Yeah. She's okay – she's knows how to handle stock."

"No ... I mean how's she doing since what happened ... you know ... the accident?"

"Oh," Chris turned sullen. "She seems okay but Charlie says she's sitting on the brink."

Josh blew out a breath. "Oh ...What's he mean by that ...?"

"What's that noise?"

Josh looked up; he could just see the helicopter sitting over the trees, the roar of the fire drowning out its sound. "Look!" Then he heard the horses, their feet striking stone, scrambling. The ground started trembling. "Get aboard," he yelled at Chris. "Take your side! They're coming too fast!"

He vaulted into the saddle and spun Jesse around, just catching a glimpse of a wall of flames rising through the trees, very close. "Get ready to fall in behind them, Chris, and if they break away, leave them, get the hell down the gully and ride hard. Look!"

Chris's eyes grew wide open – the flames were almost on them. "Hell! Where'd that come from?"

As much as he wanted to bolt hell for leather into the gully ahead of the bolting herd, he trailed out the whip and waited, shaking, sweating, yet talking soothingly to Monty, who would want to be amongst the front runners where he usually worked. This was not going to be easy. He thought he heard shouting, Clarrie's voice drifting through the smoke. "Clarrie! Clarrie!!?" he shouted back.

The horses reached the gateway but propped in the opening to the road, the lead runners quickly summing up their surrounds. Two riders had the road guarded, but ahead was clear and open. They charged on through, Jasper almost at their head like a Judas goat. Chris's heart lifted that it was all going to plan. His heart pounded loudly at the glorious sight of horse after horse leaping over the fine line of where tarmac met vegetation, then pounding on through to continue down the Overflow.

Then came the first of the cattle, lumbering with good winter fat, horns keeping their personal space as they fought for a space through the gateway. And that's where it all turned to shit. They didn't hold their line. Spreading out to gain more space and to stop being jostled from the runners behind in the rush to save themselves, they spilled out onto the roadway and spread out; some missed the gateway, though some went on through. About a dozen trotted away up the road, inciting others to follow.

Josh sent Jesse after them on his side but realised if he relinquished his space, more would escape around him.

"Hold your line, Chris! Don't leave your space!"

Chris also swung back to where he'd been standing as more cattle poured through.

As more cattle broke around him, almost knocking Jesse over, Josh let fly with curses. He cursed himself further for losing concentration as the helicopter rose above the trees. He knew they would have to be getting out of there soon as the flames were almost on them. Maybe it was only the helicopter's downdraft forcing back the flames.

Any moment he hoped the Herefords would appear, and Clarrise and Bawldy. They would need to start running real fast into Blackfield, though he doubted they would have time to save anything but themselves when they got there. He hoped his mate Charlie had gotten out. But he doubted too that Charlie would have gone and left Chris and Clarrie behind.

The least they could do was save the Herefords after all this, for Clarrie's sake, and for Kate Norton's sake.

Just then the cattle that had scooted around him, the ones he had kissed goodbye and left for the fire to claim, came loping up behind him, causing Jesse to tuck her tail and run a few steps forward. She spun to protect her hindquarters, and Josh let out a whoop of joy.

Behind him, the road was filled with fire trucks coming towards him through the smoke, and the verges had turned into yellow barriers walking beside the trucks. The firefighters had come, and were sending the cattle back their way. And up behind Chris, through the pall of smoke, came more trucks and more firefighters, all droving cattle. The cows fell back into the herd, turned, slipped in through the gateway and galloped off down Benders Gully. Holding their place well back, the firefighters began reeling out hoses and lining up along the road.

The first of the Herefords came trotting through, black streaks on white faces telling how close the fire was.

Clarrie plied the stock whip over Bawldy's rump screaming up at the sky: "No! No!!" She could see the shooter stiffen, meaning he had his target and was about to pull the trigger. She couldn't stop it. She couldn't get over Bawldy and stop the shot. As best she could she stayed beside him, waved her arm out across the top of him trying to cover every inch of him at the same time. She waited for the retort, waited for Cascade to leap out from under her at the sound, or tangle up with Bawldy as he toppled over and over. "No!!" she screamed again, unaware of the tears streaming down her face. *"No!! Please God no!!"*

She didn't even realise she'd prayed; prayed when she'd told herself all those months ago she would never pray again. There was no God. God couldn't be so cruel. But now … for Bawldy's sake …

Coming up the valley just behind the tree line, Allee Lang worked at making her father proud. "A new fire has broken out about a kilometre ahead of the main fire-front and has spread across Benders Gully. We can only hope the herd is ahead of this new fire front. As you have just seen, as we came up the valley, the stock trucks are about an hour from Blackfield where folks are already evacuating ahead of this fire. So far, six of these small mountain communities have been overrun by flames, this being a severe weather phenomenon on one of the hottest, driest seasons in a century. There is just so much fuel on the ground out there; nothing is going to stop this disaster until it is ready to stop."

Lew swung the camera round as they climbed up over the trees.

"And there down below us … yes … yes … we can see the herd! And they are running, folks. They are tearing down the mountain. I can't see Chris yet. But there, there is Clarrie Darcy driving them from behind. And … Lew … Lew, look over there … what's going on?"

Lew zoomed in on the helicopter hovering above the gully, hovering above the tail runners of the bolting mass of beasts. "He's got a rifle," he said to Allee, honing in on the shooter. "He looks to be aiming at Clarrie, or the herd …"

The pilot, without instruction, swung the aircraft in a wide arc and came up on the shooter's side so Lew could focus directly on him.

The shooter shielded his face and withdrew back into the cabin. With a few choice words in the pilot's ear, the pilot hoisted the helicopter high above the trees, high above the smoke and swung away over the mountains to cleaner air.

The air space now clear, Allee picked up the megaphone and yelled down at Clarrie: "Go, Clarrie, go!" as the flames leapt high behind her.

Her face stained with tears and streaked with falling ash, Clarrie separated the reins again and backed off on the rushing, panicked bull. She tried to breathe in deeply but the painful lump in her throat was slow to clear. She stood in her stirrups to stay with Bawldy and to keep Cascade well in hand, maintaining just enough pace to stay with the bull and outrun the flames.

As they broke through the gateway a roaring cheer went up along the road and she felt a soft cooling spray mist all over her.

"Go on, kids," one of the firefighters sooled. "Get this herd on home. We'll hold the fire here as long as we can."

Leaving the cheering firemen behind, and there must have been fifty of them giving them precious time, Clarrie ploughed on through the gateway behind Bawldy, Chris and Josh falling in behind her.

At a slow loping canter that Cascade seemed most controllable at, Clarrie noticed Josh and Chris loping up beside her.

"The gates have been opened at the next road and the firies said they will have it manned to push the cattle through. It's a straight run through to Blackfield now."

Clarrie simply nodded, slightly annoyed yet accepting that she had prayed; and awed yet confused that her prayer had been answered. She looked up as the helicopter zoomed across the top of the gully and headed south down the mountain.

∾

CHAPTER TWELVE

Back in Blackfield, Charlie had left Nanna in charge of tending the hot animals inside the truck. After ensuring the ground support man at the stand-pipe frequently flooded the cab and canopy with water for her, he strode off to prepare for the arrival of the trucks. On his way across the town, he asked for directions from numerous folks. Many patted him on the back, some almost consolingly that he was losing his brother and sister to the fire.

"We've got trucks coming up," he explained to two elderly gents standing on the verandah of the local store. "I just need to know where is a good place to load them from."

"Sale yards," jawed one.

"Showground," said the other.

"Sale yards got more loadin' ramps," the first argued.

"Showgrounds better. Got loading ramps at different areas. It'll give you time to draft the stock for loading. Them cows got horns?"

"Some of the Herefords have," Charlie offered.

"Well, if they've got horns and they're coming fast, they might get hooked up in the sale yard lanes and pull others down. That'll jemmy up the works."

The other old man nodded.

"I been loading stock around these parts best part of forty years. Showground's your best bet."

The other man nodded again and left his friend to it.

"Now a pup like you, sonny, looks like he could do with a hand to get your livestock loaded …."

"Aren't you pulling out with the rest of them?" Charlie asked, noting more and more cars leaving town.

"Soon, but we don't want to sit around on the side of the road waiting while those idiots sort 'emselves out. Old Bessie there will get down best if she can coast most of the way." He indicated a battered brown square-nosed pickup parked near the store. "We've had a good life, kid," the man added, noting Charlie's surprise, "we don't need to rush." He stepped down off the verandah. "You coming, Bert?"

Bert stepped down and followed, his legs shorter and a little more bowed than the first man's.

"Name's Ed," the man said, reaching over and shaking Charlie's hand. "You kids are doing a fine thing saving that stock on the mountain. We been fighting the government for years to get more stock grazing up there in the Park. We live here. We know what needs to be done in the ranges to prevent this happening, and that is grazing down the feed to a reasonable level, then these fires wouldn't get away. Too late now."

Charlie noted the man had a distinct limp and lifted his shoulders when he walked to give him lift. He looked awkward and the man noticed him watching.

"Old war wounds," he half laughed. "Got gored by a north-west bull in the Kimberley bout twenty years ago. Snapped my hip in two places and it never quite healed." Then he got down to business and sent Bert off to commandeer the Showgrounds. "Started drovin' by truck after that."

Charlie couldn't bear the thought of rounding up cattle by

bike instead of from the back of a horse. He'd tried it once or twice but there was just no point to it – nothing raised the heartbeat more than the solid run of a horse in full fight, with your heart beating in unison. Nothing beat the feeling of a horse moulding itself under you and veering into your slightest weight shift.

"You come from good cattle blood, Charlie Darcy," the man said bluntly, his weathered hand landing on Charlie's shoulder.

"You know who I am?" Charlie sounded astounded.

The old man half laughed again. "Sure do. You're Kate Norton's grandkid. I remember you lot, all of you kids, tearing up and around the park on your little ratty ponies, spooking all the brumbies. I'd say to my wife every time your folks packed up that truck and took you all home 'Gwen, there they go – all survived another season.'"

Charlie grinned. He sort of knew what the old man hinted at. He, Clarrie and Chris had been going out trying to round up the brumbies ever since they could ride, and when they couldn't find the brumbies they practiced on Nanna's cattle – when they were out of sight of Nanna. Bawldy was just a calf at the time. A snake got his Dad about six years ago making Bawldy the last of a long line of Berwick Hereford bulls, which made him close to priceless. He suddenly thought that if Nanna wanted to put him up at stud she could bank roll rebuilding her house.

"Well here's the sale yards, son. See what I mean about horn trapment? Not a good place to run excited, horned stock. And you'd have to load each truck separate."

He proceeded around the sale yard fence line to the local showgrounds beyond. A set of wide, high double gates opened onto an area of seating, a gap in between leading into the sprawling grassed oval. "Show grounds and rodeo," Ed said, "which makes it perfect for your purpose."

Ed stopped walking; pointed out four areas where stock could be penned and loaded, long, high ramps with high sides rising from the pens. "What have you got in that herd? I only been hearing news reports on the radio."

"From what I saw flashing by in Moreton, about fifty brumbies, a hundred odd mixed Angus belonging to Jake Coskins, Nanna Kate's herd of thirty Hereford ..."

"Did you get all the brumbies, son?" Ed looked keen.

But Charlie shrugged. "I don't know. They just poured down out of the park and joined the Herefords."

"Did you see a big chestnut stallion in amongst them?" The old man's eyes had moistened.

Charlie looked at the man, not sure what to expect next; thought he'd better get it out in the open straight away. "We've been trying to catch him for years. We came up here in particular to catch him this trip." But the old man wasn't interested in Charlie's plans.

"Was he with the herd, boy?"

Charlie nodded, and the old man started walking again, nodding to himself as he went. Finally, when Charlie caught up with him the old man turned. "What were you going to do with him if you caught him?"

Charlie's back stiffened. "We're going to breed from him ... raise and break the foals ..."

Ed started walking again, heading for the back of the arena where the pens and ramps stood silent. "I see you kids are doing everything possible to stay afloat," he said solemnly, "even hair-brain schemes like this."

"There's nothing wrong with Flaming! He throws a damn good foal," Charlie objected. And there was nothing hair-brain about their plan.

"That he does, but it ain't because of any blood of Old Regret's, if that's what you think you're onto. I been saying for years he ain't by Old Regret, nor Old Regret's sons. Regret was a brown. And a brown would have trouble throwin' a classic chestnut like that one. The odds are so far against it, it ain't worth countin'."

They reached the area where the trucks would arrive, where they would back their trailers up to the ramps. It was open and clean, plenty of room not to interfere with each other while they prepared for the loading.

"No, boy, that horse is by a big stallion called Moonfire, bred from a top racehorse ten years after Old Regret's colt passed on. And a better bloodline than Regret's. And you know how I know …?" He had Charlie's full attention. "Because I put him there. He was my horse …" he banged himself on the chest, "… when I had me accident and I couldn't ride again. … I couldn't bear to think of someone else getting on him and ruining him so I turned him loose up on the mountain. He's sired some real good types up there – and that big liver is his grandson, the spitting image of him. Can you believe that?"

Charlie waited for the old man to lay claim on the horse that was to be the pride of Spur-Lea Stud. But the old man simply sighed. "You look after him now. I trust you kids will look after him. He's gonna be right nasty though that he's lost his freedom." He huffed another breath then said: "Right now we gotta start organising how we're going to load these babies. We gotta separate the horses from the cows, and the horned cows from the hornless cows. Can't have them doing damage to each other on the drive. And we gotta separate that stallion.

He goes on the same truck as his mares but separate. We gotta get ready, boy, and there ain't much time to do it."

"What I want to know is," Charlie aired the biggest worry he'd had since walking over to the showground, "…how are we going to get the herd out of Benders Gully and across here without losing them?"

The old man's lips twisted with thought. "Hmmm. Now that's something we have to think about."

Further over in town, to the side of the school oval, vehicles pulled in and out of the local Fire Brigade facility. Voices coming over the radio drifted on the wind, the steady delivery of news or instructions calm but undecipherable to those in earshot. Ten trucks, all fully laden with water, pulled out one after another and headed out of town, five in each direction. A row of cars, now the way was clear, filled up at the service station across the road, the owner putting it on a tab for later payment to ensure everyone could leave town. He left the tab on the counter under a rock. If the fire came through and burned the remaining fuel, it would burn the tab as well. He could claim it all on insurance. If the fire bypassed the town, and the tab stayed intact, he knew the residents would come in of their own accord and settle up. That's how it was in the country. Nanna Kate queued up to fill the truck's tanks as well, hoping Charlie wouldn't panic if he returned and saw the truck gone. And she bought Shy an ice-cream, also on the tab.

As she parked the truck back amongst the trees, noting many of the cars quietly pulling out of town now the fire trucks had left again, she noticed the news reporter standing on the oval turning circles, searching. In the next instant, she struck off towards the Fire Station and disappeared inside.

Klemm Dodson's gold Four Wheel Drive was parked out front, and the man strode out a short time later with Allee Lang snarling at his heels. Nanna Kate was too far away to hear the conversation, but there was one hell of an argument going on over there. She guessed it looked pretty much like the arguments she'd often had with Dodson, except Alleena was jabbing a finger up at the sky above the mountain.

The young woman's long blonde hair flowed and swung with her snappy head movements, making the fight seem even more ferocious. She turned and stormed away from him, heading back across the oval, but only gained three strides before she turned back and landed a smarting blow across the fat man's cheek. Then she turned and stormed off again. Dodson stood looking stunned, his hand holding the heat on his face.

Now that the truck was back in place, Allee Lang headed straight for her. "Hello, Nanna Kate. Do you know where Charlie is?"

The old woman shook her head. "All I know is, he left little one with me and went off to organise trucks or something."

Allee breathed with relief. He was getting ready. As they'd flown back in to Blackfield she'd seen the trucks only about ten kilometres away. They would be here soon. She surveyed the hills again and by the heat on her face knew the fire would be here soon as well. She looked for evidence of the wind change but knew it hadn't come; saw Lew heading her way, camera cases now hanging around his neck, weighing him down, all 'nice-to-have' equipment stored in the helicopter they had now sent back to the city out of the fire zone. She would encroach on the truckers for a lift as she wanted to stay with the herd and follow the story through, and she would make sure the kids stayed with her to get their story.

She stood with Nanna Kate looking up at the mountain and the flames and smoke now obscuring the hills and trees in total.

"I spoke to the Fire Chief over there," she told Nanna, hoping to ease her mind as much as she could. "Those fire trucks that just left are heading for Barton Road. Another contingent of firies linked up with the kids up on Chesterly Road and helped them keep the herds coming down the gully. A fire sprang up pretty close to them but they are fighting that to give the kids more time. These guys that just left … they are going to have the gully open ready for when the kids get there and make sure all the stock continues down on this last section. They said the kids are fine and they'll be here soon."

Nanna Kate remained silent. She'd been through fires before, but this one was too close for comfort. Anything bad could happen at any time.

"We've got a few spare minutes, Nanna Kate. Can I do an interview with you, something we might use at a later date? The public is going to want to know how all this eventuated; what the kids are like, that sort of thing."

"Why'd you hit old Klemm Dodson?" she asked, her jaw tightening.

Allee's own jaw set. "Let's say I followed a hunch." She signalled Lew to start the camera rolling.

&

CHAPTER THIRTEEN

Down on the flats at the base of the mountains, at the Royal Agricultural Society showgrounds on the edge of town, Minnie Watkins strode about chucking orders at the volunteers. "Get two more pens erected over there and make sure there is somewhere to keep any stallions away from the others. There'll be another influx in here shortly."

She continued her authoritative walk towards the office she had commandeered to aid organising a shelter to receive evacuated livestock from the fire zone. Already a hundred horses stood in the Showground's stalls and more were being trailered in. Right now, though, she had a media interview to attend, and mentally prepared herself, even though her mind was halfway between needing to organise someone to erect more shelters on the open space for the livestock coming down off the mountain and especially where she could contain the truck load of brumbies.

She smiled, realising the cameraman was filming her coming across the grass.

She stopped beside the reporter. This was the third media shoot since midmorning so she knew the drill: Look at the reporter and refer to him by name – Gary – give him a rundown of how things had been going since the fire began then look at the camera and give the message she needed people to know. She glanced back at the hills in the distance; the whole top of the mountain was obscured by thick rolling clouds, and out of that cloud coursed a long line of vehicles, some heading her way.

"Hello, Gary." She smiled a little grimly.

"Hello, Minnie." Gary turned to the camera to talk to the viewers. "We are here now with Minnie Watkins who is running the animal shelter at the Merrimbee Showgrounds. What's the situation here now, Minnie? You had fifty horses come in from the evacuation last time we spoke."

"Yes, Gary, and that number has now doubled and more are coming in. We still have room and can set up temporary pens if we need to. What we do need is buckets and feed bins. Many people just didn't have time to get those belongings out. We are also calling for donations of hay and chaff if anyone has supplies they are willing to bring in – these people have lost everything and only had time to get out with their lives. Please …"

"Have you heard of the situation up on the mountain with those two young riders driving down cattle and horses in front of the fire?"

"Yes, Gary. They are very brave kids and we are praying they make it through. Right now we are preparing pens to take on the brumbies if they make it out and Merrimbee's Horse Rescue is ready to take them over after the rescue. So we are managing here for the moment, Gary. We just need feed and buckets as a matter of urgency."

The reporter wound up the report, signed off and he and the cameraman wandered off to look at the kennel area where dogs and cats were being contained.

"So how do we know the brumbies are coming here?" a young woman sitting on the step of the office asked.

"Where else are they going to go?" Minnie said haughtily.

The woman pulled back with stunned surprise. "And what happens to them then?"

"Each of our squad will take one home if they want to and we will home out the rest to families to care for. Why?"

The woman shrugged. "I just half expected they would end up at the sale yards once the truckers get them loaded. They must have some plan for them seeing they risked taking their trucks up into the fire zone."

Instant deliberation crossed Minnie's face. She hadn't thought of that. "I'll organise someone to go up and make sure the truckers bring them here. We are the rescue organisation and them ending up in the sale yards is no rescue at all." With that, she strode off to find a strong-minded person to drive up and take charge of the herd on its arrival in Blackfield.

Meanwhile, up at the Blackfield showgrounds, Charlie answered his mobile phone. He'd been ignoring it all day at the odd times it had rung.

"Charlie Darcy,' he said sullenly, knowing the number instantly. "It's not a good time to talk right now, Mr Bradley. … Yes, I know the situation and we are doing everything in our power to correct it. Spur-Lea was left to us by our parents. They own two-thirds of it and …" He shook his head adamantly. "We are only three weeks behind. We have a way of getting on top of it. No! … No, you have to give us time."

Karl Bradley, on the other end of the line, refused to agree. He had given them a time to be out of the property – a date to vacate, which didn't give them the time they needed to break a few horses and make some sales. On top of that, old Sam Coskins had moments ago tracked Charlie down and thanked him for saving his cattle, cattle he now had no means of supporting. So he'd given Charlie the herd. The Darcy's had saved them, he said bluntly, the Darcy's could look after them. Sam Coskins had lost everything and with his farm burning to the ground he had no means of support to agist the cattle anywhere either. If Charlie didn't take them they would go to the slaughter yard, which Coskins hoped to avoid. So Charlie had even more reason to keep control of Spur-Lea.

But the Bank Manager wouldn't budge on the date. They had two months to vacate and the property was being foreclosed on. Nice doing business with you, Charlie!

Charlie stood stunned, his eyes seeing Ed and Bert organising people in the arena, but his mind not registering anything but the problems he now faced. He had these horses and he had these cattle, he just didn't have anywhere to keep them long term.

His hands clamping tight to the back of his head, he turned a circle trying to visualise a solution. How would they survive as a family if they didn't have Spur-Lea? And where would Nanna Kate go? He'd vaguely thought she'd come with them, and he'd deal with the edginess he'd seen between Nanna Kate and Clarrie when that bridge had to be crossed. A lump rose in his throat – now none of them would have a place to go.

"What's wrong with you?" Allee Lang jibed as she reached him. "You look like you've eaten a worm."

Charlie swallowed thickly. "We've just lost the farm."

She scowled and shook her head. "Spur-Lea? Oh, Charlie …"

"The bank is foreclosing. We've got two months to get out. Saving the horses has just posed us a whole lot of serious problems."

Allee rubbed his arm consolingly. "I'm sure they won't go through with it when they know what you are going through."

"They know. They know we spent every spare bit of cash we had on a lawyer to stop them turfing us out on our ear when our folks died. Then they just hounded us and hounded us. It's over now."

Her attention averted to the arena where men hurried about pulling down panel fences and temporary pens. "What's happening here?" she asked.

Charlie shrugged. "The old bloke, Ed, is getting things set for loading the trucks."

Allee nodded – that was good. "The Incident Controller said the trucks are about ten minutes away. How are they going to get the cattle from the gully gate into the showgrounds?"

Charlie shrugged again. "Beats me. I don't even know if Ed knows that one."

"Well you'd better come up with an idea pretty quick. They're not far away now. And nor is the fire. I heard through a firie's truck radio they have crossed Barton Road." Then she proceeded to tell him about Klemm Dodson and the sharpshooter trying to take out Bawldy on the run. Charlie turned pale.

❦

CHAPTER FOURTEEN

Up on the Overflow, embers continued to rain down around them and the heat brought sweat to horses and riders, the air so hot it had become harder to breathe. Clarrie, Josh and Chris had long bouts of coughing just trying to draw enough air to breathe. Bawldy snorted frequently and had slowed his pace considerably; he'd even stopped once or twice and took some heavy persuasion to move on again.

"You might have to consider leaving him," Josh posed the solution. "It's no good if you both die trying to save him."

Clarrie's teeth clenched and her nostrils flared. "Nothing is going to burn, Josh. Nothing is ever going to die by fire while I'm breathing," and she laid a resounding whack on the bull's red rump to make her point, striking the bull much harder than she'd intended. She rode on in silence ahead of Josh to keep the bull moving seeing the whack had made an impact.

"He'll have a heart attack if she keeps pushing him," Josh shouted to Chris. But Chris accepted Dead was Dead, one way or another and Clarrie had decided it would not be by burning. He pulled the handkerchief up around his mouth again and urged Monty on after her. Josh followed, concern now for the bull and what was going to happen when they reached Blackfield. They had over two hundred cattle and fifty odd horses, all running together. He felt he should ride ahead and warn them they were coming but it would be too late — he wouldn't be able to get far enough ahead of the herd to make a difference, and at that speed it would put Jesse at risk. He patted the brown mare and loped on after Chris and Clarrie.

Ahead, Clarrie crowded Bawldy and watched the sky. The area ahead was open and she feared the helicopter would return and make another attempt to shoot him; she needed to be close to do whatever she had to do to stop it. But all she saw in the sky was black smoke and floating embers and all she could hear was the roar of the flames behind her consuming everything. The fire had been about a kilometre behind them for most of the way, maybe further now if the firefighters had managed to slow it down at the road. But the intense heat and the amount of ash and glowing leaf litter falling around them she doubted they had stopped it. The fire wouldn't be satisfied until it had eaten everything on the mountain. She prayed Charlie had everything in place in Blackfield for she was too tired to ride any further, and Bawldy was not up to running any longer. She prayed he had it in him to reach Blackfield.

That's when she heard the louder roar as flames sprang up beside her. She screamed and gripped the reins tighter as Cascade bolted forward then veered to avoid the flames that flared beside him. "Hurry," she screamed at Chris and Josh. "Hurry!!"

Behind her, Josh cracked his stock whip and the herd in front of them leapt into a gallop, even Bawldy. The race for their life down the mountain had begun again as flames sprang up all around them. The terrifying roar drowned out all other sound, growing louder as the flames tore higher. They were still three kilometres from Blackfield.

Allee Lang followed Lew across the showgrounds as he sought out a vantage point for filming the loading of the stock.

The phone in her pocket started ringing and she pulled it out, checked the number. 'This should be good,' she mused, showing Lew the number. "Yes, Dad."

"What are you still doing up there in the fire zone? The helicopter arrived back half an hour ago. You promised to be on it. I want you to get in a vehicle and get the hell out of there. That fire is roaring down the mountain. You've got to get out now, Alleena."

"Dad, you have no idea what is going on up here. We have to capture the full story … these kids …"

"I don't care about … well I do care about those kids, but I want you out of the danger zone. I'm sending the helicopter back for you."

"It's not safe to land and take off from here now. And the horses will be here before it arrives. Lew and I will jump a ride on one of the trucks. We could be out of here before it arrives."

"I don't care, Allee. The last report just said the fire has jumped again and is only an hour from Blackfield. I want you out of there. That whole damn mountain is going up!"

"Yes, I know. We can see the flames flaring up at times but, Dad, this story is more than two kids droving a herd of cattle down the mountain. You have no idea who this family is and what they've been through. They need our help." She started coughing as the wind blew through, bringing with it a huge, thicker draught of smoke. "I was talking with the kids' grandmother a while ago and you have no idea what they've been through. We can't just abandon them. You know, they had to spend every cent they had to make the bank allow them to keep the farm left to them in their parents' estate and now they've run out of money the bank intends to foreclose. And there's more, Dad … how's this for a reason to stay here …

Nanna Kate is …"

She prattled on, hoping it was enough reason to appease him, seeing he'd allowed her to take on the primary reporting role, even if it was all a matter of circumstance. Flying over the ranges on their way back to the city, she had tapped Lew on the shoulder and indicated the flames crossing paddocks way below them. Instantly, Lew had picked up his camera and started filming. Anything was better than the mundane assignments they'd had to cover so far, he'd said – Alleena being the face of social news media and knowing she also wanted more. Last night's wedding of a tycoon to a woman a third of his age had been a dull affair, but they'd been put up in a classy hotel in the hills to ensure it gained media coverage. Nevertheless, they were both glad to be on their way home. Seeing the fire, she had phoned her father.

"Dad, have you received any reports of a large fire in the hills to the north? It looks big, and there's a couple of towns directly in its path. Is Paul or Jeff coming up here to cover it?"

Lew had swung around to see the response on Allee's face. As an 'in-the-area' cameraman he might get a chance to film something important for a change. She shook her head, mouthed, "They're both out of action," and Lew swung back to film more of the raging flames sweeping through the forest ahead of them. The pilot immediately diverted from their straight line to the city and flew a wide arc around the scene, enabling Lew to capture some poignant footage for the night news if the fire proved a problem to the area.

"Lew and I are here already. It would be better to have something rather than nothing, wouldn't it?"

There had been a long pause while Leo Lang lay down the law to his twenty-two year old daughter who was trying to break into the world of news reporting.

"Human interest angle only," Alleena had said, repeating her father's instructions. "And not too close to the fire. Gotcha … And get the helicopter out of the area before it's placed at risk. You got that, Dillon? Got it, Dad. We'll give you live feeds as long as we have reception then store footage, and have the helicopter back before dark."

She hoped there would be enough importance for him to forgive her, for him to realise news reporting ran in her blood and that a good story came above everything.

Meanwhile, at the back of the Community Hall, Klemm Dodson stood red-faced, glaring at the sharp-shooter who had missed the shot. "What the hell am I paying you for?" he jabbed the man in the chest. "You were supposed to take out that bull so the old lady has no rights to the high country. You couldn't even do that. Well you have one last chance, sport. This time you'll take the shot and I don't care who gets in the way. We're coming back to rebuild and I want full control of the high plains."

"I'll be in place. But I won't be shooting unless I have a clean shot," the man retorted.

"You'll shoot, damn it! You will take the shot!"

Then an announcement came over the loudspeaker system at the oval. "Attention everyone! Attention! Traffic is clearing on Tumble Creek Road. Everyone prepare to evacuate the Centre. Please get in your cars and wait for the signal to leave. Do not overtake on the journey downhill. Trucks are still on their way up and the right lane is blocked by them. You will only cause a traffic jam. Keep to the left at all times. Anyone prepared to hold back as long as possible to assist with the loading of the cattle and horses your help will be appreciated."

On the mountain road, trucks growled as they climbed the steep ascent, hugging the right lane to avoid the traffic descending. Horns tooted, and passengers cheered and waved out their windows as they passed.

"Looks like they're keen on us getting there," Joe said over the two-way. "How far out are we?"

"About ten minutes," Stu replied.

"And where are we going to load up?" Lennie asked.

Silence came over the radio for a moment. "The sale yards, I reckon," Joe advised. "It's best set up for penning."

"We won't have time to do this thing if we go to the wrong place, guys," Stu added over the air.

"There's only one other place I can think of to load and that's the showground. They are both on the same road so just keep coming. Take the right hand fork as you come into town, Mac."

In the blue sedan following the trucks, Max Ryan from the Merrimbee Horse Rescue Association received instructions from his superior.

"Don't take any nonsense from them, Max. If these truckers think they can hone in on this haul of horses they've got another thing coming. You know the rules and so will they. We expect to see you at the showgrounds with those horses within the next two hours."

"So what's going to happen to those the shelter team can't take?"

"We'll hold them for a while to make sure they're okay then let the Brumby Association have them. That way we'll all get an influx of funds when we tame them down and sell them on. Then everybody will be happy. We'll even claim back the trucking costs from the Disaster fund so we're not out of pocket. Just let me know when you are on your way back."

Max rang off, preparing mentally for the battle he would have with the truck drivers who were trundling towards Blackfield in front of him.

Up in Blackfield, men and women scurried across the arena, hauling, shuffling and resecuring yarding panels. Bert stood out on the road watching traffic flowing out of town at the fork. The heat had become unbearable and the air was thinner than usual. He had tied a wet handkerchief across his nose and mouth but it had done little to break up the smoke that now burned his eyes. More cars had started moving around at the Community Centre, everyone ready to pull out and make a run down the mountain. As time drew on and the flames on the mountain stood more pronounced and the heat singed everything around him, he doubted the kids had outrun the fire. He wondered how long Ed intended to stay and work at getting the animals loaded, animals that probably wouldn't arrive – the fire was so close and the gully run so treacherous at this end where it gradually narrowed to the gateway, one cow down on the run at that point would take down all those behind them, blocking the way of the others to the gateway, blocking in those kids as well. Regardless, they should have been here by now.

Lew stood off to one side, watching Bert and ready to film the convoy of trucks coming into town. Every bit of footage he could gather would contribute to the documentary Allee had started talking about. She would never be given a scoop over her brother Paul but she had enough friends in the studio to help put it together. The more footage he could gather for her, the better – he did, however, have to be sure he was present for the herd arriving in Blackfield.

At that moment, as the wind blustered up the mountain, he heard the deep, throaty growl of engines above the roar and crackle of the fire. His camera hoisted onto his shoulder, the boom mike directed out in front of him, he called Allee over and started the camera rolling. Sure enough, through the smoke haze appeared the chrome grill and blue body work of a Kenworth prime mover. Above the cab rose the slatted surrounds of the double-decker stock trailer. Two trailers. He filmed its approach, and its passing, then swung back to catch the red framework and dusty grill of a Freightliner, also a double-decker with twin trailers. The engines reowwed down as Bert stepped forward and directed them into the rear parking area of the Blackfield Showgrounds. Another blue truck followed, then an orange Freightliner. Bringing up the rear line was a white Volvo. In the lens of his camera, Lew caught it all, each truck powering up the slope through the smoke, then gearing down for the turn and swinging into the back of the arena, Bert waving them forward towards Ed. He swung the camera to Allee, who made sure the trucks were in the background.

"This is Alleena Lang on site at Blackfield, a small mountain town in the direct path of the Alpine Range wildfire. They are expecting the fire to arrive here within the hour and we are still waiting for the herds of horses and cattle young Chris and Clarrie Darcy are driving down the mountain gully to safety. You can see behind me the trucks arriving. These trucks will transport the cattle and horses down the mountain to safety. But first the herds must get here."

She started to walk across the arena. "This is the area the herd will be shepherded into and split into beasts of kind. I've been told that if they are not transported correctly they could suffer critical injuries from the other stock so they need to be, I believe the word is 'draughted' into separate areas. Apparently, this will take some time to achieve and you can see behind me a number of local residents have hung back from evacuating to help get this done." She noticed beyond the white arena slats and railings an official looking car pull up beside the trucks, and while Ed was trying to get the trucks in place at the loading ramps, the drivers were called to attend a meeting. She needed to get across there to find out what was going on, but right now, she was on air.

"We expect the herd to be arriving at any time and know that at the last sighting about five kilometres up the mountain Chris and Clarrise, and another unidentified rider, are still driving the herd ahead of the fire front. The problem now is how they will hold the herd together to get them from the Overflow across to the front gates of the Showgrounds. If they can do that they will be channelled down the alleyways around the grounds straight into the main arena. This is where the draughting will take place.

"We can see flames rising high on the mountain not far from town and have been told this is the last area in Blackfield to evacuate. We hope that won't be too long happening as the flames, the heat, the wind, it's phenomenal here, and red glowing debris is dropping all around us. You can see the sparks flying out of the darkness here. You can't imagine how dry the air is and how hard it is to breathe, and those young riders are closer to it than we are. It is becoming increasingly dark as the smoke completely covers the sun on this stifling, hot, summer's day that will be the worst in Blackfield's history.

"And so we wait for the arrival of the herds. We'll be back with more live coverage shortly. This is Alleena Lang, National News Service, reporting direct from the Blackfield Showgrounds."

As she lowered the microphone, Lew stopped filming. "Something's going on over there, Lew. Let's find out what."

Briskly, they headed across the arena, by-passing locals erecting panel fences, the arena now almost divided in two across the short side and divided again towards the centre from the farthest end.

Out in the parking lot, five truck drivers gathered around an officious-looking man who seemed to be laying down the law. Allee signalled Lew to start filming and wandered closer to listen. The drivers didn't seem too happy.

"As I said," the man reiterated, "you don't have stock movement permits for any of this stock so legally you need to be careful what you do. Under rescue circumstances, I believe you can do whatever you like with the cattle," the man said, "but those horses have to be delivered to the Animal evacuation centre at Merrimbee Showgrounds. They are trained to deal with these issues and will ensure they are suitably homed."

Two of the truck drivers shrugged. "It makes no difference to us," Mac said. "We've just come up here to help get them out."

"We should really talk to someone about what the plan is for the stock," said Lennie.

"You can lay claim to them for the cost of coming up to get them out," Max Ryan prompted.

"Hey, come on, you guys, we need you in position now. They'll be here any minute."

The pack broke up and headed for their trucks, Ed directing each to where they would collect their stock. The trucks roared back to life and arced around to reverse up to the loading ramps. Gates were opened ready to receive. Then Ed gathered them together out of ear range of the official, informed them of who would carry what. That's when Allee went forward to also put her information forward and to get a seat in one of the trucks for her and Lew.

Across from the showgrounds, Nanna Kate, sitting in the front of the truck, noticed the sharpshooter heading into the scrub beside the gully. She looked for Charlie but he was talking to an old bloke at the gateway to the Showgrounds. Shy had fallen asleep in the front seat and the cab had been so thoroughly hosed down if there hadn't been an outlet in the truck for water run-off, it would be like releasing the forty day flood when the doors opened.

All the cars had been moved and lined up ready to pull out onto the mountain road, the truck carrying all Nanna Kate's possessions amongst them.

About ten minutes from the gully's end the horses cantered strongly, the chestnut stallion flanking the lead mare and pushing her on. Behind the mass of bay, grey, roan and red rumps pounded rippling bodies of brown, ash and chocolate — Coskins' cattle — their hides foamed with sweat, amongst them creams and brindle Wagyu. Then a gap to the Herefords, all orange and white, lumbering along, heads low to the smoke.

Right on Bawldy's tail rode Clarrie, the folded stock whip tapping him when he fell back, Cascade bowling along head arched, many strides almost on the spot. He snatched the rein frequently trying to stretch his bound but Clarrie stayed on the stirrups, holding him together.

Chris came up beside her, Josh tailing him. "The fire is getting pretty close, Clarrie. We should leave Bawldy behind and save as many as we can." He coughed violently, smoke engulfing his throat. His eyes moistened his cheeks which were now crimson from the heat.

"No!"

"Clarrie!"

"No!" she almost bellowed at him.

"But…"

"No! Nanna hates me enough already – I can't let her lose Bawldy as well."

"She doesn't…"

"Yes she does!! Now you and Josh go ahead – take the herd as fast as you can. I'll catch you up in Blackfield. Besides you have to get down and make sure that gate is open. If the herd gets there first you won't get near the gate to open it. We'll be stuck."

"I'm not leaving you, Clarrie."

"Yes, you are, Chris. You've got to do this," she shouted. "You've got to make sure we can get out."

Fear struck Chris's blue eyes.

"I'll see you at the bottom. Josh, go with him."

With that, Chris urged Monty faster, but Josh remained, little Jess bounding to keep up with the mighty Cascade. He just kept staring at her.

"Go, Josh," she hastened him. "And be ready to catch Bawldy at the bottom. Even if we lose the rest of the herd out of the gully you and Chris must be ready to catch up Bawldy."

Josh nodded, awed that logic and planning was still occurring in her pretty head.

"Be careful at the bottom. It's very rocky and narrows to the gate – you only have the width of the gate to get through. Water flows beyond that point into two huge concrete pipes and goes underground – comes out further down the mountain beyond Blackfield. I don't know if the pipe is fenced but it's probably full of debris and you won't get through. Push Bawldy to the gate and you'll be fine."

She nodded. "Go! Look after Chris."

"Okay, but you stay safe," he said.

In another moment, he had given Jess her head, and the mare had sprinted away down the wash.

Clarrie was alone again. Her nose stung with the acridity of burning bushes behind her and the constant ignition of tiny embers beside her.

Bawldy kept plodding along, relentless trotting that covered little ground and she knew she had run his heart out. She noticed the gully narrowing slightly; flicked a smouldering leaf from her hair; noticed the singe marks on Bawldy's hide.

"Come on, Bawldy. You've got to run. Nanna won't survive without you." Flames leapt up behind her. "Come on, run! You're not going to burn."

Further down the gully, Josh caught up with Chris. "Keep your eyes peeled for shooters, Chris."

Disbelief filled Chris's eyes.

"My dad will do anything to stop your Nanna having grazing rights to the high country. I saw shooters up in Moreton but they didn't get off a shot. Blackfield will be their last chance to get Bawldy so be ready."

Chris nodded, his eyes scanning the bush.

"The gully's narrowing, Chris. We are nearly there! When the horses break into the open we need to be on their right to turn them towards the Showgrounds."

"Do you think we can hold them?"

"If we don't, we have to let them go. Bawldy is the one we have to keep."

They were now level with the horses and sprinted ahead.

"Get your whip ready," Josh yelled. "Use it as you need to."

They burst through the open gateway, and both peeled to the right, the lash of the stock whips dragging behind them. A moment later, the ground shaking, Flaming surged through the gateway, and his herd erupted into the open spaces of Blackfield.

About four hundred metres back up in the bush, the shooter poised on a rock above the gully, ready to complete his mission. One shot, and he would benefit big time. Whether he took out the bull from a helicopter on the cull or from a vantage point at the side of the gully mattered little to him. He raised the rifle, took aim as the orange-coloured herd started loping by.

On the outskirts of the showground, Ed gathered his people. It had been years since he'd organised something like this – in his later years, he had worked on stations mustering and helping load the stock trucks for trips to the port. In his retirement, he'd organised the showground; and assisted with stock management at the rodeos. He was surprised in these few hours just how much he missed it.

He scanned the area. "Okay, is everybody ready?!" He thrust the gates wide open, gazed down the long laneway formed by panel fences and vehicles on one side, a row of men with stock whips on the other. The vehicles would stop their run to the west, the sale yard fence and unmounted stockman controlling their run to the east.

He could feel the earth moving. "They're coming!" he yelled.

At the back of the arena, truckers climbed the railing to watch the herd arrive. Klemm Dodson stood behind a gate at the far end of the arena, watching in the hope the great Hereford bull would not be amongst them.

Lew propped himself on the front bonnet of a truck, adjusted his camera to the darkening conditions. Everything now had turned eerie. It was mid-afternoon but looked like dusk. A red sun hung in a black sky barely visible through the heavy layers of smoke. Flames threw red lines all across the hills bringing a colossal amount of red to the scene. Wind blew furiously low to the ground, scattering red specks like a metal grinder going berserk. He caught it all.

He caught Charlie standing on the hood of his truck wiping smoke-induced tears from his eyes. Charlie, a small child clinging to him – the big brother-father figure and he was only twenty-four.

He caught Chris and his offsider bolting into the makeshift laneway, surprise on their faces that they were set up again by the goodness of the locals hanging back to help. They galloped forward, sprinted down the race lying flat against their horse's necks, Charlie cheering as they passed. Then a silent pause of nothing. No one speaking. No sound at all, except the rumble. A strange foreboding filled the air.

Then, out of the heavy smoke came the stunning liver chestnut, leaping and careering at the closeness of man. It powered on after the riders. More horses streamed by in his lens. Charlie whooping again as a big brown horse with leather headstall pounded by in full flight. Then a big black, also with headgear, set the child to leaping up and down on the bonnet, denting the metal.

Dust competed with the smoke, competed with the glowing embers.

Lew sat ready as in burst the cattle, not as fast but jostling each other as they hugged the centre of the raceway. One or two drifted and the loud crack of stock whips sent them back. Stockmen silhouetted by red glows, spattered by pinprick embers - this was the best filming of his life!

Cattle poured on past and just kept coming, more than he had estimated from the helicopter earlier. He heard the clang of metal gates; men shouting, the lowing of beasts as they were turned back from wrong areas. He swung the camera, caught footage of the first trailer being loaded.

He caught the fire trucks, their red pulsing lights adding further eeriness as they pulled into the car park near the trucks; caught others pulling alongside the line of vehicles that formed the raceway. Leaping down firefighters hauled on the hoses, swung them out across the ground and laid them ready.

"The fire is on the ridge behind the trees. Everyone get ready to go," they yelled.

Lew caught Charlie; captured his worry as the last of Coskins' cows bustled through and all that was left was darkness and smoke and a dull red glow. Long, long moments passed.

Then white appeared, white pinned to broad orange heads, then orange bodies. The Herefords trotted sedately through the gate, unflustered by the flurry of activity and human contact. Again Charlie punched the air. He could see him shouting: "Yes! Yes!"

The cattle trotted on down the raceway, like the end of a fun run, and disappeared into the grassed arena, backing off slightly as men began to direct them. Lew could hear the commotion going on in the showgrounds. Now loud clomping as cattle scurried up the loading ramps. Whips cracked, the urgent need to move stock where they needed to be eradicating niceties.

Lew caught Charlie still watching the gateway out of the Overflow. Watching. Watching. But the raceway remained empty. Charlie leaping down from the bonnet, hoisting the child and tossing her back into the cab. Charlie running towards the gateway.

Suddenly through the gateway came a massive grey horse, bounding forward with enormous strides; perched on its back the teenage girl, her face smudged black, her hair blowing in the strong wind. She hauled on the reins in front of Charlie; rubbed the smoke from her eyes.

"Did Bawldy come through?" she shouted through the darkness. "It's so thick out there I couldn't see."

"No," Charlie yelled back, shaking his head. "But you'll have to leave him. There's no time. Everybody's pulling out before the fire gets here, and it's right on us. Come on, Clarrie.

Get Cascade loaded."

"No! I won't leave him!"

Charlie grabbed for the reins but the girl had already spun the horse around and had bolted back to the gateway. She disappeared through the smoke and was gone again, Charlie sprinting after her. Lew kept his camera on the gateway, glanced back over his shoulder where the two boys on horseback were helping to move the herds to the make-shift draughting lanes; men separating horses from cattle; Angus cattle from Wagyu cattle, Wagyu from Herefords. The stallion careered around the arena, agitated at the loss of his herd and his close confinement amongst humans.

He swung back as Charlie sprinted, shouting, "Clarrie! Clarrise!" He almost reached the gateway but stopped, looked back at the truck, at the small child leaning out through the window. Embers fell like glitter over the ground. His hand on his mouth, terror in his eyes, Charlie turned back.

Firies yelled across the raceway, yelled at the vehicle drivers. "Come on! You've got to get out of here. Lead car, get moving."

Car engines started. Windscreen wipers cleared debris and ash to improve vision for the drive. Lew brushed falling litter from his shirt and hair. He could feel his skin burning. It was time for him and Allee to be moving. He heard a loud retort that echoed through the bush, and re-echoed, ringing loud and clear above the roar of the fire. His head turned towards the gully. It sounded like gunfire.

Chilling at the thought of what they'd seen before, he shook his head. Surely, no-one would be daft enough to be up on the slope near the fire trying to get the bull. But what else could it have been? he countered.

Maybe one of the cars had backfired. Though the sound hadn't been that close.

He pushed the thought aside, hoping it was nothing yet felt suddenly sick. One last shot of Charlie ambling back, turning, wiping tears from his eyes. This was just awful. This wasn't supposed to be the ending. This was all going to destroy the kids, the story, everything. Now it would be all over the news – Stupid Child Sacrifices Life for a Cow. Now he was sorry for all the footage he had taken of the brave fight that had been fought to save the livestock. Was the life of a child worth it? Viewing Charlie's anguish, he knew it wasn't.

Then Nanna Kate was in the raceway, grabbing Charlie, shaking Charlie. Yelling. She started running towards the gate, more a quick shuffle than a run but he knew what she intended. On the hill to the north of town flames shot high into the darkened sky, the heat robbing oxygen from the air, making it hard to breathe. Firefighters waved cars forward, directing the flow towards the road. The trucks were almost loaded, only the cavorting stallion resisting leaping onto the ramp.

The laneway was dispersing, Charlie now chasing Nanna Kate, grabbing her and turning her around, hugging her. Tears stained their faces. Tears streamed down Lew's cheeks. Then Allee was there.

"Come on, Lew. We've got a ride in the trucks. They'll be pulling out soon. The firies are just hosing them down to wet the cattle for the drive down the hill. Come on!" Then she noticed his face.

"The girl hasn't come through. Well she came through then went back into the smoke. She hasn't come back yet."

Allee's face paled, fell blank as if she was trying to fathom what was happening. What it meant.

Movement to her right turned her head. The silhouette of a man running towards the arena, the rifle in his hand horizontal as he ran. He came from the scrub near the gully. Instantly Allee knew.

"Oh God, Lew. Oh no!" then another thought. "Film him, Lew. Get him on camera."

But Lew had already hoisted the camera to his shoulder; he captured the silhouetted man on his run, zoomed in to enhance detail. Then the man was gone. He swung back to Charlie and the old lady. Charlie clung to the truck door, grief beyond logical thought. A fine spray of water swung around the scene causing steam to rise from the ground, from the vehicles yet to move. Steam replaced smoke. Lew shielded the camera.

"You've got to get Charlie moving out of here. He's not going to want to go, you know that."

"He has to. The fire is going to consume everything."

Meanwhile, up on Benders Gully, Clarrie veered back and forward through the bushes and rocks, heading for the last place she'd seen Bawldy. She'd tried to call him, but smoke filled her mouth on each call, and she'd almost been unable to breathe. As it was, her throat was so parched she wanted to throw up. But she kept searching, reining Cascade left and right, the big horse snuffling and shaking his head.

When flames sprang up ahead of her she screamed, the fire so close now she doubted she could outrun it. She also screamed as Cascade spun from the flames and almost dislodged her. If she came off now she would never make it out of the gully. But as the big horse spun on his back legs and almost took control of the rein, she glimpsed a patch of white over near a fallen tree. It was Bawldy and he was down. Her heart hit her boots and she kicked Cascade across the distance. If Bawldy was gone her Nanna would hate her more. And what a sad way for such a magnificent bull to go. She knew it was her fault. She had pushed him too hard; she had kept pushing him down the mountain. He'd probably had a heart attack, or suffocated on the smoke. Tears filled her eyes. And for the first time she realised just how much she'd loved that big orange beast. She'd grown up with him and the rides she'd taken up on the high plains had been as much to check on him and see that he was doing okay. Now this. This just wasn't fair. She'd done everything she could to keep him safe.

She reined Cascade in. She didn't want to see Bawldy like this. She didn't want the last sight of him to be this bad. She started to sob. As large blobs of leaf litter rained down she knew she had to leave him.

Tears flooding her eyes, she murmured, "I love you, Bawldy. I'm sorry. I'm so sorry."

Smoke billowed across the space between them, almost obscuring the big white face that stretched on the ground between his front legs. She turned Cascade to make a run for the Showground. She had no right to destroy Cascade as well. And wasn't it uncanny that she would end up the same as her parents, burned to death – though not by a petrol tanker explosion – but by the bush she loved so much. One glance back at Bawldy before she left, she urged the dappled grey to move. He didn't take much urging. But as he bounded forward she saw white movement from the bull. His head had lifted. She reined in abruptly and swung back. Sure enough, the big bull shook his head and bellowed deeply.

"Bawldy, get up! Come on, you've got to get up!" But the bull just heaved a sigh and snorted smoke from his nose. "Come on Bawldy!!"

The big bull looked up at her – clearly he'd given up.

"Come on, Bawldy!" Her voice was almost a scream as she almost lost control of Cascade again. Any moment he would haul her forward and be off, with or without her, and her hands were so torn from his constant snatching she could barely hold the reins. There was nothing else for it. She released the lash of her mother's stock whip and let forth a resounding crack to the side of the bull, the first time she'd ever threatened a beast so chronically. It had the effect she needed and Bawldy stumbled to his feet.

Once again, the epitome of the blessed stockhorse, Cascade wheeled in behind him and the race was on for Blackfield. In the short time Bawldy had been down, he'd regained some stamina and now he bowled into a run. Down the gully he lumbered, easing up only to scramble over rocky ruts or slight inclines. The fury of the fire was behind them and spurred them on.

"Not far to go," Clarrie told the horse and bull. "Come on, it's not far to go."

Down in the arena, the last few head of cattle bundled up the loading ramp. Gates clanged, beasts bellowed as embers rained down on them. More sprays of water poured through the slats, putting out the skin-torturing litter. "Come on, you've got to go," the firefighters yelled. "Everything is going up. Get these trucks out of here."

Chris and Josh loaded Jesse and Monty into the back of a high-sided flat top, single layer, pushed them into a space and dropped their bridles off. Then Chris turned back to the arena.

"Where's Clarrie?" he bellowed. "Where's Clarrie?"

"Come on. Let's go back for her," Josh yelled back. Before he could run two strides, a heavy hand clamped on his shoulder.

"No, you boys get in the trucks. There is nothing you can do for anyone out there and if we don't go now everyone here is going to go up in flames. Come on, you in there," Ed directed Chris to the truck moving Coskins' cattle.

"I can't leave her out there," Chris protested, but the man strengthened his grip and turned him towards the truck, and he didn't let go until Chris started climbing into the cab. And he stayed until the cab door had shut and the truck was moving. That was the second truck to move out.

Josh stood for long minutes watching the gates to the arena. A tower of flames as high as a building built a wall of death that steadily consumed the world ahead of it. His heart thudded heavily. It wasn't fair. How could she die like that when she'd saved so many? His eyes moistened more from his grief than the smoke.

"Come on, son. Your ride's moving." And he was physically guided to the cab and pushed onto the front seat beside the driver. As the truck started rolling forward Josh's face pressed to the glass in the vainest hope that Clarrie would appear.

Allee clung to Charlie's arm, also in disbelief that the fire had been cruel and taken the girl who had saved so many lives. There was no way she could survive the fire on the hill that was roaring their way. "Charlie, you've got to go. You've got to save Nanna and Shy. Follow the trucks down. I'll be in a truck behind you."

Charlie's face was balled in grief, his tears eradicating the burning smoke that almost blinded him. Almost sobbing openly, he took Nanna Kate's arm and turned her towards the truck. "It's not fair. She shouldn't go like our folks went. She shouldn't have suffered like that."

Wetting cloths in the overflowing water trickling from the truck, he placed them over Nanna's and Shy's mouth to reduce the amount of smoke they were breathing and reluctantly climbed into the cab. He had a responsibility to the living. It was something embedded in him by his father, Martin Darcy. *Save what you can. Do for the greater good.* He put the truck into gear, embers scurrying in all directions around them as it started rolling forward.

"Come on, Lew," Allee yelled. But Lew was still filming, filming the devastation, filming the heartache, filming the human reactions – it was easier to deal with it through the lens of his camera than in reality. He panned the hills once more. Though his skin was burning, this one final shot would be a reminder to all how a young girl had died in the flames, sacrificing herself to save the helpless beasts on the mountain. 'This is her heartland,' Charlie had told him. 'She's like her Nanna in so many ways, and her heart belongs to the high country.' If he was interviewed at any stage over this whole experience, that was what he would remember about young Clarrie Darcy – her heart belonged to the high country and that was where she died.

He was about to turn off the camera and run for the showgrounds when movement through the smoke caught his eye. He was good at picking detail and kept the camera rolling. "Allee, look!"

From out of the smoke came the trundling big red bull, trotting steadily, its white face now sooted to darkness. A sharp crack sent it loping across the open space. A few moments later, into his lens came the enormous grey horse cantering, bounding, and shaking its head violently to shake away its controller. The girl on its back stood braced on the stirrups, a short rein easing the horse left then right to keep the beast on a direct line to the showground gates. Embers flew out of their way as she streamed down the now gone raceway, almost filling his lens with a giant grey blur. He swung down and followed her passing till she disappeared into the arena. Then he turned off the camera and ran after her; ran after Allee.

In the showground, more gates clanged as the last cattle truck closed up. The driver headed for the cab, keen to leave the fire zone. He'd never expected when they'd decided to come up to help that they'd be racing the fire all the way down the mountain, running for their lives. He was more than thrilled that the cattle had loaded swiftly and he could now be away. He turned the key, ready to pull in behind the already moving rigs. As he engaged first gear he noticed the old man who'd organised the loading leaping up in front of his windscreen, waving his arms frantically. He wound down the window that he'd kept up to keep embers from igniting the interior.

"You've got one more! The bull's just coming into the arena."

"Too late," the driver said. "We'll be burned alive if we don't go now."

"It won't take a second to load him."

The driver shook his head.

"Well I'm not stepping out of the way until he's on board," Ed professed. "Come on, man. You're wasting time talking. Let's get him loaded."

Cursing, Stu flung open his door, slammed it shut again and ran for the back of the trailer. Sliding back the barrier, he positioned himself to reset the gate the moment the bull was aboard, loaded into the space that had been kept vacant just for him. He noticed the bull on a direct run down the length of the arena, the young rider he'd heard the news reports about dogging his heels, her body pitched over the horse's neck as she bowled along behind him. Bloody good rider, he thought, noting how she managed the monster of a horse with barely a movement of hand or leg. And she had the bull on a good run that would send him straight towards the ramp to his truck. He had nowhere else to go. "You little beauty!" he yelled at her. "Keep him coming."

He noted Joe in the truck beside him standing ready to receive the monster grey horse, which would be loaded into the second last slatted space – only two gates to close and he would be away as well. He noted Joe was just as wet with fire hose spray as he was yet could still feel the heat through the moisture. He noted too there was just one other horse in the arena, a magnificent chestnut stallion that ran frantically about trying to find a way out of the high white railings. He would need to jump seven foot if he was to escape the flames for they had tried repeatedly to send him to the ramp but he'd been too nimble and too determined about not being confined. He would die amongst the flames – there was nothing else for it.

"Come on, kid, bring him straight up," he beckoned, watching her direct the bull straight down the line. Then he noticed from the corner of his eye the high wide gate to the side of the loading bay, a gate that gave access out of the arena, had began to swing wide open. Handling the gate was a stout, balding man in smart jacket and moleskins. He'd seen him lurking around behind the chutes while they were waiting to load. So what the hell was he doing?!

"Hey, you, shut the bloody gate!" he yelled down at him. "Shut the bloody gate."

The bull was so close now he had no time to climb down and swing it closed himself; he had no time to do anything. And the bull had now deviated and headed straight for the opening, and so had the brumby stallion. *Geez, that would be two now trying to outrun the fire while they were trying to get down the mountain.*

Standing back against the railing, Lew kept the camera rolling, Alleena standing to one side of his shot so he could capture the final loading. Her face glowed red, reflecting the approaching flames.

"We are here now," Allee reported as Clarrie bowled past her, "the last of the stock to be loaded and the fire is just about on us. If the bull loads well we will be heading down the mountain in a few moments. And I can't tell you how keen I am to get out of here. This heat is intense, I can feel my hair is singed and my cameraman's shirt is starting to melt. We simply cannot hold up here much longer. Cars have already hit the main road down and away from Blackfield, probably the last time many of the locals will see this place, many of whom have grown up here."

She noticed Lew shift the camera and alter the zoom. Turning, she almost cursed "What the ..." She saw the arena gate swing open. "Oh no, the bull is heading for the open gate. Oh no, not after all that has been done to save him. And the big brumby stallion the kids call Flaming is also heading for freedom. Who opened that gate?"

Lew zoomed in further and picked up the form of Klemm Dodson heading off towards his Four Wheel Drive, the only person in the vicinity.

"Oh, this is tragic," Allee rued.

As the white barrier beside the truck slowly opened, Clarrie's heart fell to her stomach. She screamed out: "No!" but it was too late – the gate was pulled wide and Bawldy and Flaming both had their sight set on it. Both picked up speed to gain space away from the fire. Instantly Clarrie gave Cascade rein and her heels, and he plunged forward. She lay low over his neck and gave him his head. In one bounding stride, he had flattened into a gallop, his neck stretched and his eyes glimmering at the challenge of working a beast at speed. Hugging the arena fence, she gave him room to run and room to turn; she knew she had to get ahead of both bull and steed and slam the gate shut before they reached it.

But Flaming also sprinted; he matched the giant grey stride for stride and, for a moment, Clarrie couldn't guess if she or the stallion would reach the opening first, the bull some long metres behind them.

Allee watched wordlessly, awed at the skill of the girl and the power of the horse as they skirted the arena wall in a flat-out run. Cascade gained strides on the stallion and, as he almost reached the opening, Clarrie swung across it and, hauling suddenly back, she stood in the stirrups as the giant dappled grey slid across the gateway on his hocks and reared up high in the opening. But the stallion kept coming, unperturbed by the solid wall of flesh blocking his way.

As Cascade's front feet pawed the air, Clarrie unfurled her mother's stock whip and swung it over her head. She brought it down with a sharp and sudden crack that retorted loud across the hills and filled the arena with an urgent, deadly threat. The stallion slid to a halt; stood wary, trembling, staring her down as Cascade grounded his feet and stood stock still, his neck arched, waiting. The stock whip lash lay loose in the dirt as Clarrie glared back at him.

Then Charlie was at the gate, closing it. She caught a glimpse of Nanna through the truck window; she was staring at her, crying, while Shy bounced on the seat with elation.

"I got him, Charlie. I got him."

And Charlie was crying openly, hugging her leg as she sat with the stock whip still loose and ready.

"Are you getting this?" Allee whispered to Lew. Practiced, Lew kept the camera focused, pulled his head back and nodded as Allee stepped back into the frame.

"This is truly amazing. I've never seen anything like this in my life. A young girl facing down a wild stallion, saving a prized bull from the flames, she truly is Clarrie of the Overflow, and I have been told there is indeed a close family tie to the famous namesake."

A sudden gust of burning wind blew her hair forward and the air began to sizzle. "Right now, we are going to get out of here. The trucks need to get onto the mountain road and away before the wooden trailers begin to burn. We need to get the livestock to safety."

Behind her, Charlie had taken a stock whip from the fence and tapped the red bull back towards the loading ramp, and Bawldy lumbered up meekly into the confines of the trailer. The gate clanged shut, and Charlie turned his attention to the stallion. As the mighty grey turned to face it down and Clarrie teased out the lash along the ground in front of the stock ramp, Charlie blocked Flaming's run back down the arena and left him only one choice — the one loading ramp left available. Seeing horses ahead of him, Flaming bounded up the ramp and scrambled into the truck, the driver swinging the partition gate closed behind him. He signalled Clarrie to bring up the head-tossing grey. Dismounting, Clarrie tossed the stock whip to

Charlie and ran with Cascade up the slatted ramp where, inside, she dropped his bridle off and swung out again. There was no time to tend him any better than that.

The back of the truck secured, the driver indicated for her to climb in the cab, shovelled rubbish out of the way so Alleena Lang and the cameraman could take up the back seat, and in seconds he had the engine barking to life. As the truck bucked into action, the firefighters beside them waved them off with a lifesaving spray of water then they too leapt aboard the pump trucks and smaller fire tenders and pulled out after them.

At the far end of the showgrounds the wooden railings began to steam then crackle and burst into flames. Soon, Blackfield would be nothing but a black memory.

In the truck heading down the mountain, Joe introduced himself. "You did a mighty fine job, kid. I've not seen anything like it in all my years hauling stock."

But Clarrie was too tired to talk; too worried about Nanna Kate in the truck ahead of them. She turned to Alleena in the back. "Did Chris and Josh get in alright?"

Allee smiled and nodded. "They're in two of the trucks up ahead. We now just have to get down the mountain before the fire."

"You should ring your Dad," Lew prompted. "He's going to be hell mad that you stayed here this long."

Allee nodded, wishing to delay the call. He would be furious with her whether she rang now or later. She reached forward and stroked Clarrie's cheek. "You're burnt," she said.

"So are you," came the reply.

And they both smiled.

Behind them, the flames hit the trees around the showground and all was swallowed by flames.

CHAPTER FIFTEEN

"So what made you come up to help?" Allee asked Joe as he turned onto Tumble Creek Road. "You guys are a blessing in disguise. Saving the stock was impossible without you."

Joe glanced at his wing mirror at the height of the flames rising on the hill behind them. "We work with stock all the time and you just don't want to see any harm come to them, not like this," he said. "And when we saw that kids were doing their darndest to save them, we knew somebody had to do something."

"So what was the argument you had with that guy in the stock yard?" She knew some heavy words had gone down with the man.

"Who? That guy from Horse Rescue? … He told us the horses have to go to the evacuation shelter and the Animal Evacuation group will take them over. The cattle we can take wherever we want but the horses are Horse Rescue's responsibility."

Clarrie's jaw dropped and she and Allee retorted simultaneously: "What?"

"Yeah. Lennie and Steve said they will take the cattle wherever they are wanted, but the horses have to go to the Merrimbee Showgrounds."

Clarrie's stomach dropped, and her heart thudded heavily. Lost for words, she could only shake her head.

"You can't do that," Allee fought for her. "These kids, Clarrie, Chris and … Josh? …" she caught Clarrie's nod, "risked their lives to bring the horses down. Clarrie's brother Charlie told me they intended to truck them to Spur-Lea where they would be tamed and broken for riding. What has the Horse Rescue group got to do with it?"

"I dunno," Joe shrugged. "I just know we were ordered by the powers-that-be that these horses have to go to Brumby Rescue."

"What happens, Clarrie, if you don't get to keep the horses?" Allee asked pointedly.

Tears welled in Clarrie's eyes. "We lose Spur-Lea. We have no way of supporting ourselves and we will lose the farm. We lose everything Mum and Dad worked for."

Concentrating on his driving, Joe fell silent.

"And what about the stallion, Clarrie?" Charlie had told her of their plans in those long hours of waiting but Allee needed Joe to hear it from Clarrie.

"We were going to use Flaming for stud – keep the best of the mares and breed from them. We've been watching Flaming since he was a foal – it's like he has always been ours."

When Allee started to ask another question Joe said: "Can you guys be quiet - the stock is moving about and I have to concentrate to make sure we make it down the mountain."

And that thwarted Alleena's subtle plan to change the driver's mind. She fixed her eyes on the road ahead, shivering as small spot fires started up on the verges as they passed. She gazed out the back window, caught glimpses of the convoy of fire trucks following them down. She knew she should be phoning her Dad but decided to do so in private – she was going to get one hell of a roasting when they talked next and she didn't want it to be in public.

Four trucks ahead, as they rounded the bends, Chris kept checking in the side mirror that Clarrie still followed. He worried for her and he worried for the horses. All around them embers dropped from the sky and the smoke over the road made it slow going. He feared the fire in the hills would overtake them and kept watching as flames ripped skyward, flaring high in the blackness.

"Can't we go any faster?" he'd eventually asked the driver.

Lennie, his lips drawn to a fine line as he concentrated on the road, had responded: "I'm going as fast as I can, kid. Any faster and we might just end up off the road. Besides, I can only go as fast as the truck in front, and he can only go as fast as the truck in front of him."

Chris had remained silent after that, until they had hit a series of sharp left and right hand turns. The cattle jostled in the trailers trying to keep their footing, their movement causing the trailers to sway. "Have you got control of this thing?"

Lennie chuckled. "Yeah, kid. This is normal. As long as we keep moving forward the trailers will sort themselves out. It's speed that takes them off the road."

In the third truck, silence reigned, Josh also trying to gain glimpses of Clarrie in the stock truck at the back. He had nothing but the greatest admiration for her now – that on top of the feelings he'd been trying to fathom since they'd met in the high country years earlier. And he didn't know what made him keep a subtle watch on vehicles passing through Moreton, until now – he'd been watching for her – watching for the Darcys to come visiting. And he'd especially watch at the change of seasons when they'd come en-force to drive the Clancy cattle off the plateau and down into the gorges for winter protection.

This visit had caught him unawares for the cattle had already been driven up to the good grazing land for the summer. How glad he was that they had been there, for Kate Norton would certainly have perished in the fire. It was then he realised, for the first time, just how much they had lost. They had all lost their homes – he'd lost his battered up ute that had meant the world to him; it was his independence – he'd lost his job for there was little work in Moreton at the best of times, everyone running family businesses to survive, and now the herds he had tended for the Jacksons, Coskins and Milners were gone. He shuddered at the image of the herds that didn't escape – how had they fared? Had it been quick? Had they escaped? At least this lot had made it out, he blew out a breath. And the horses had made it out. It was a good thing Clarrie and Charlie and Chris were doing, giving them the chance at a new life. Sure, it wouldn't be the same as having the freedom to run wild in the high country but they would be fed and sheltered and never suffer the harshness of the elements. And the Darcys would make sure they were placed in good homes.

He thought then about the big stallion he'd always wanted to catch but who had eluded him every time he'd given chase. The last he'd seen the big horse was eluding all attempts to load him – he hoped they had at least opened the gate and let him loose rather than let him suffer a horrendous death in the yards. Then he thought about Jesse – he had sacrificed his ute to bring her out and she was worth every cent of the loss. With her, he could eventually head up into Queensland and see if there were any jobs on stations – that was about the limit of his thinking right then. His Mum would undoubtedly stay with her sister from this point on – they had nowhere else to stay – and his Dad … well his Dad could go wreck himself.

Josh flung himself back against the seat. What a sad realisation it was that his Dad was an intolerable man! All those years he'd stood by him, listened to his dreams of opening up the high country to campers and tourists, of building a big resort at Mountain Peak where people could hire horses and enjoy the national park like the Clancy's and Darcy's had when they'd owned the land. The old cattle way stations would have been rest points for lunches – how he had planned at the dinner table all the things he would do in the high country if he could just get Kate Norton's cattle off the land. And, of course, she still owned the cattle way stations. But they were all gone now.

Josh wondered where his father was now – the last he'd seen him his dad had been watching the loading of the cattle through the back showground gate. He'd be a man without a cause now – gone from a Shire President with big plans to nothing. Josh frowned deeply. How desperate he had been to secure the high country lease … had he really secured the shooters that stood on the cars down in Moreton ready to drop the cattle. Had he employed the shooter in the helicopter that went after Bawldy and put Clarrie at risk? He didn't want to believe it. He couldn't believe it. But something rankled him deeply. Why had his dad hung out in town when the fire burned down on them? Why hadn't he raced home to get his mother to safety? Being wheelchair bound, she had no chance to do for herself. He himself had raced home and packed her bags and precious things ready for his father to arrive but the man never came. He never came. It was Josh who had driven her down to Blackfield and sent her off with the buses that were evacuating. It was he who had rung her sister to collect her from the Evacuation Centre. Then he had driven back and rescued Jesse, saddling her to ride her out for he had no other means of transporting her. He'd heard on the radio that Clarrie and Chris were bringing the herd down the mountain so had waited and joined them. It was because of them Jesse was on the truck behind coming out with the rest.

On the mountain Chris had told him of their plight and he was glad Clarrie had been there to rescue the herds she could. He smiled remembering how dirt streaked her face was; how tattered her hair had become; how singed in places. He bet she had no idea how rough she looked.

Only now did he realise how tired he was and how much Clarrise Darcy played on his mind. He doubted he would see her again after this for their lives were about to head in different directions.

Leaning his head back, he closed his eyes. They were painful and felt full of grit. And he listened to the hum of the wheels on the road.

In the truck ahead of him, Chris felt gobsmacked. "No," he said tightly, "we need those horses. We came up here to get them and take them home. Especially the stallion."

"Can't help it, son. The man from the Rescue Association gave strict instructions the horses were to be delivered to the Rescue shelter, and that's what we have to do."

"It's not fair," Chris argued. "*They* weren't up there saving the horses. Why should they have them? And they don't need them. Don't they get funding and stuff? If we didn't go up there to save them, they were going to be shot in the wild horse cull anyway. Our plan was always to hide the herd so none of them would be killed. What was the Rescue Association doing to stop that happening, huh?"

"What cull?" the driver's interest peaked.

"It was planned for two days' time. The helicopters and shooters were already in town and had flown over a few times checking out where the herd was. And they usually have instructions to drop as many cattle as they can as well ... my Nan's cattle," he added. "And who was protesting to stop the cull? Not a peep out of anyone. At least we'd have found them homes. And my brother breaks horses in real gentle. They would have made nice riding horses. Now we're gonna lose the farm, and Charlie won't be able to tame any more horses. And we'll all be split up by the government because we have nowhere to go."

Lennie just listened – remained silent for a moment. Then said: "And if you get the horses…?

"We'll start our own stud. That Flaming is a top horse – he'll sire some real beaut foals. And with our own stud farm we'll all be able to work together and get out of debt. It's what my Mum and Dad dreamed of."

"So, where are your folks in all this?"

"They got killed in a car accident six months ago,' Chris said glumly. "A petrol tanker ploughed through them at an intersection. That's why we had to round up the stallion so we could find a way of keeping the farm." And that's all Chris could say.

Another long silence as Lennie remembered the news reports of that horrendous accident; how the tanker's brakes had failed on a downhill run; how it collided with a Four Wheel Drive, spinning it around, rolling it over; how the teenager in the back seat had been flung from the vehicle before everything burst into flames. Tragic. "Your sister ... she the one who survived?"

Chris nodded, unable as yet to speak much about it.

Lennie leant forward and picked up the microphone to the two-way.

"Stock convoy on the mountain, this is Hulking Hauler."

Four drivers responded briefly.

"Guys, you know how we're supposed to deliver those horses to the shelter …? Well, we're gonna drive right on by and take everything to a place called Spur-Lea." He glanced across at Chris, whose eyes had brightened even through the smoke-induced redness. "Yep. Everything goes to Spur-Lea."

"That bloke from Animal Rescue is ahead of us. Isn't he going to be waiting for us at the bottom of the hill to escort us in?" Steve asked.

"That's the plan. We can follow him," came the reply.

A whoop went up in the trucks forward and back, and they rolled on down the hill, smoke swirling away as they rumbled through the bush.

&

CHAPTER SIXTEEN

At the rear of the convoy, Alleena pulled out her mobile phone and made the dreaded call to her Dad, updating him with all that had happened and was happening on the drive down the mountain. Repeatedly, she assured him she was fine while hoping to avoid him for several days till the scorching on her face diminished.

"Dad, these kids are being shafted from every quarter. They've got the bank foreclosing on their home; they've got this Animal Rescue group trying to claim the brumbies they'd gone up to save; their Nanna has probably lost everything she ever owned, except the herd that Clarrie and Chris saved – Clarrie even had to shield the bull from a sharpshooter who tried to shoot him on the run down the Overflow. There were shooters everywhere on the raceway through Moreton. ... Check the footage – Lew caught it all. ... Yes, I'm fine.

"Dad, have you bothered to watch any of the footage we shot at all today? ... Well, that's great, Dad! Thanks for your support. I don't care ... ... I don't care ... you can hand it over to Paul. Right now I need a film crew out at their farm for when they get there. It'll be a great follow up seeing the stock unloaded and settled in after the hard run they've had. And I think there'll be some altercations at the end of the run. I've heard you have Reuters and NBC and CBN all screaming for more, so we have to see the story through. And it needs to be a positive ending.

"I don't care. If Paul wants the scoop, get him there with a film crew. He can take it over – we just have to do what we can to get these kids some help. We'll be at Spur-Lea down by Lake Nadine in about three hours.

"And do something for me, Dad … if you watch nothing else, take a moment out of your precious day to watch the interview segment we did with the grandmother. This is not just your ordinary, everyday, run-of-the-mill great cattle roundups of all time – there's a hell of a lot more to it."

The trucks barrelled on down the road, fire trucks now passing them going in the opposite direction. Ahead, the long line of cars slowly thinned as Blackfield residents diverted to family or friend's homes or to one of the various shelters across the city.

Lennie picked up the microphone. "We're coming up on the Showgrounds, and that bloke is out the front signalling the way in, Joe." He hit the horn and gave the man a hearty acknowledgment, and kept going. So did the next truck with the Angus cattle, its air horn also blasting three times. The horse truck with Nanna Kate's Bess and all her geese and goats and sheep, and Shy-Lee's little Pebbles followed, silent: the horn hadn't worked in such a long time. The third truck hit the horn and Stu gave the man a regal wave as he drove on by, as did the Hereford transport, also giving a loud series of horn blasts. Then came the truck with the horses he waited for. Barp. Barp, Barp. And on by went the brumbies, and the stallion, and the five Darcy stockhorses, and the little bay stockhorse, Jesse.

Josh and Chris, in their trucks, glanced back to see the man leaping about and shaking his fist in the air.

"Not happy, Jan," Josh quipped, laughing.

In Lennie's truck Chris kept watching in the side mirror. "He's getting in his car. I think he's coming after us."

"Not much he can do until we stop, kid," the driver said.

And the convoy roared on heading for Spur-Lea, that sprawling acreage around a crystal blue lake west of the burning hills.

As conditions allowed along the highway, the brumby transport overtook the cattle trucks until it led the convoy, the Brumby Rescue vehicle blocked well in behind. Joe quizzed Clarrie on the layout of the farm – where do they unload? – how much room was there for trucks their size – what was the paddock layout, the fence construction? Clarrie answered all his questions, kept a check on Cascade, Monty, Jasper, Titan, Jingo and Jesse. Three were in amongst the brumbies, then Monty and Jesse in another partition, then Flaming. Cascade was in the rear compartment. She thought about Josh and all he had risked coming back to get Jesse. She didn't know many boys who would sacrifice their car for a horse. *Come to think of it*, she thought, *I don't know many boys who liked horses either*. She liked Josh Dodson though, even though she'd tried not to. He must have known what his father was up to, trying to take out Bawldy, and she'd argued with him up on the high plains many times about it. He'd argued back that the high country was for everyone, not just Kate Norton's cattle. And she'd jibed him that Nanna Kate didn't restrict people in the high plains – she didn't care as long as they left Bawldy and his herd alone. She'd often seen Josh riding in the national park, many times standing on a hill looking down at the brumbies below – he'd never interfered with Nanna Kate's herd and she should have thanked him for that. More than that, she realised, she needed to thank him for his help down the mountain. They probably wouldn't have made it without him.

She also realised how tired she was — she'd been on the go since the early hours of morning and it now was late afternoon. She touched the tender places on her cheeks and arms; she felt burnt, and shuddered at how her parents must have felt when the petrol tanker ignited and erupted in flames. Flung from the car, she'd not seen a thing until waking up as they'd loaded her into the ambulance. How could it be that she had a mere concussion and they were both killed so horribly? She should have been there to help them; she should have done something … And all she could do now was be there for the rest of the family; help run the farm; raise Shy-Lee; make sure Chris did his homework. Shy hadn't minded her taking over the household … as long as she was fed and had clean riding clothes, saddle rugs and girths. Chris, however, didn't like being bossed about, and didn't like cleaning his room, or helping with the cooking. And he always argued why he had to. And she'd just say 'Just do as you are told,' and Charlie would usually come in and tell him to 'do as you are told.' She'd expected them to hate her for the accident: if she hadn't wanted to go to Mt Holbrook Equestrian School they wouldn't have been there when the truck brakes failed. She'd expected the sort of treatment Nanna Kate had given her — avoidance — not talking with her the way they used to — catching the harsh looks coming her way when Nanna thought she wasn't watching. Nanna hated her — and if she went anywhere near her she would walk in the other direction. There was nothing she could do to remedy the pain Nanna felt. Ella Darcy had been her only child.

A fine layer of smoke lay over the farm from the hills in the distance when the trucks finally pulled into the narrow road that led to Spur-Lea's gate. Along the way Charlie had been ushered to take the lead in the convoy. Truck horns blurted as they approached the farm. Charlie did not miss the Foreclosure Notice on the front gate as he pulled in.

An assortment of cars were already parked out front of the house when Charlie drove in, a news crew and cameramen filming the procession of trucks from different angles. They captured the loud blasting of air horns as the trucks came down the road, the drivers celebrating making it down off the mountain. Charlie swung the horse truck into a paddock through a gateway and around in a wide arc behind the house, lining it up against the row of trees to keep the stock inside in the shade. They had been on the float since early morning in hot conditions in a metal-sided confinement. He hoped Nanna realised how distressed they would be when they came off, those that were in a condition to come off. He dropped the ramp, knowing he had other places to be, yet took a moment to check that all had survived the heat. They were indeed distressed. "Shy-Lee, help Nanna get the stock off and take Pebbles to her stable, make sure she has lots of water available. Nanna, just let them all out here. Nothing can get out of this paddock. Shy can hose them all down when she gets back here."

Then he strode off to where the truck with the brumbies had pulled up into the wide stockyard and lined up with the stock ramp. The line of trucks blocking the road were now silent, except for a Four Wheel Drive at the rear of the last truck that blurted its horn to make them clear the way. It would be a while before they were able to do so, there only being room for one double trailer set up at a time. He ignored the camera crews, more urgency required in bringing the stock off the trailers and into more comfortable conditions. Many, he knew, would need veterinary care from the ember burns they'd received on the run down the Overflow and the drive down the mountain. It was money they didn't have but would undoubtedly have to find.

He noticed Allee Lang and her cameraman hurrying down the long driveway, being detained by a news reporter but waving the man aside as she hurried towards him.

"Charlie! Charlie, get the horses off the truck, quickly. Just keep doing it regardless of what happens. I'll explain everything later."

He looked up to see Clarrie on the stock ramp swinging open the gate; she swung into the trailer, slipped the bridle back onto Cascade and ran him down the ramp.

"Let Flaming off!" she barked as she trotted Cascade around into a holding yard and dropped the reins to hang to the ground so he would stand waiting for her return.

Charlie did as bid, the stallion spinning then charging through the trailer and down the ramp into the main holding yard. Sweating, Flaming trembled on being confined in the large yard with the high metal railings; wild-eyed, he retreated to the far end of the yard.

Running back, Clarrie snatched up two ropes from the breaking yard railing and scrambled back up the ramp. Fixing makeshift rope halters to Jess and Monty she clambered back down, swung them into the yard with Cascade. "Hurry, Charlie! Open the gate and let them all out! Hurry!!"

Frowning, Charlie heard the commotion start up at the front of the truck. Male voices shouting at each other. "Hurry, Charlie!" Clarrie insisted.

"Don't let any more horses off this truck!" Charlie heard the shouted order. Being so consumed with his duties at

Blackfield to get the horses loaded, and having no radio communications in the truck he knew nothing of the claim on the brumbies.

"Charlie, open the gate," Clarrie whispered up at him.

"These horses are being claimed by the Brumby Rescue Association."

At the front of the truck Alleena Lang slowed down, positioned herself with Lew beside the front fender. Her brother stood alongside her as cameramen positioned their cameras on tripods. Allee reached over and grabbed Lew's shirt and pulled him in beside her.

"Do you know this thing has gone absolutely global?" Paul hissed at her. "We're getting requests from everywhere for more news, more aspects on the human side of things. The phone's been ringing off the hook. Just follow my lead, Allee." He signalled for the cameras to roll.

"We are here at the Darcy property at Lake Nadine where the herds rescued off the high country plains have been brought to safety. With me is my sister Alleena Lang who has been reporting live on site in Moreton and Blackfield as the firestorm raged down the mountain, wiping out one small town after another. I believe, Alleena, you just made it out."

The camera swung to Allee, who looked dishevelled, her face red with soreness from the heat. "Yes, Paul. These trucks were the last to leave Blackfield and have brought out three herds of cattle and a herd of wild horses that were to be culled by helicopter in two days' time. Fire and embers poured down on us as we drove out of the area, the yards bursting into flames moments after we left. We were truly lucky to have survived. While reporting on the fires up near Shingle Dale we heard there was a couple of young riders driving a few horses down out of the fire zone and went up to investigate – we found out there were more than a few horses – they had rescued about fifty brumbies, and a herd of prized Hereford cattle belonging to their grandmother. In the ride that ensued, Chris and Clarrie Darcy saved two more herds of cattle along the way with the wildfire roaring up behind them. The Darcy family went up to the mountain with the intent of mustering the horses and bringing them to safety before the cull. That the fire instigated a rescue of a different kind is of little consequence."

Paul prompted for more: "I believe that now the animals have been rescued this young family have some issues they now have to deal with."

"Yes Paul. It seems now these young people have risked their lives to save the animals, the authorities have come in to claim the horses. You can see behind us the Horse Rescue Association officer laying demands on the family to leave the horses on the truck."

"Yes, I can see that," Paul said. "I wonder where that Association was in the days leading up to the aerial horse cull."

"Yes, you are right, Paul. Now that the Darcys have brought the horses to safety, it looks like they will have a fight on their hands to keep them."

The camera crew focused more on the argument going on in the background.

"You were told to deliver the horses to the Rescue shelter," Max Ryan growled at the driver.

"Yeah, but there are horses on here that need to be delivered to this location," the driver shrugged. "The Darcys have stock on board, as well you know."

Meanwhile at the back of the truck Clarrie pleaded quietly through the slats: "Charlie, open the damn gate!"

"Hey, you!" the man yelled coming down the side of the truck. "Get your damn hands off that gate! I am warning you …"

Charlie glared down at his tone, swung the gate quietly outward, held it back as the horses facing the opening took the lead and surged forward through the trailer and down the ramp into the dirt-floored, round yard below. The loud clattering of hooves drowned out the man's curses. Charlie swung down from the truck.

"What did you say?" Charlie asked him.

"What the hell are you doing?" Max Ryan bellowed at him.

"What?" Charlie said, confused.

"I told you not to let them out."

"Sorry, mate. I didn't hear you over the noise of the horses."

Josh in the meantime had ambled discreetly down to the back of the yards and quietly eased open the gate to a large paddock that ran down to the trees along the lakeshore. Once out into the large paddock they would be hard to catch and load again.

"Well you can just put them back on again," Ryan barked. Charlie threw his hands up in the air, realising what Clarrise had been on about. "Go on, you put them back onto this truck!"

"Sorry, no can do, mate," Joe intervened. "You said up at Blackfield not having a stock movement permit would be overlooked given the situation but they might not look favourably on us if we pick up from a location other than the fire zone and deliver elsewhere. I'm not prepared to risk it.

Besides, I volunteered my services to pick up and help in the rescue, which I did. Anything else after that will be on contract. Somebody will have to pay for the trip."

Max Ryan huffed a wordless curse.

"Oh, damn, look at that …" Joe threw his hands in the air. "They're shooting through down the paddock. I don't have time to stick around. Sorry, mate." He winked at Clarrise who now stood atop the ramp shutting gates in readiness for the truck to pull out.

"Thanks, Joe," she said.

"Take care, kid. And good job today. You're a real gutsy kid. And remember, possession is nine-tenths of the law." Climbing up into the cab, he gave Charlie a nod goodbye and pulled out, clearing the way for the cattle trucks to pull in and unload.

Alleena and Paul stepped out of the way and moved along the railing. As they discussed the situation further Clarrie could be seen in the yard behind them stripping saddles from the horses and laying them on the railing.

"It looks like that problem is over for the moment," Paul noted. Allee kept a straight face, yet internally the warmth of elation coursed through her. "But I noticed as we came into the property there's a foreclosure notice on the gate. Can you tell us anything about that, Alleena?"

"Yes, Paul. I was speaking with Charlie Darcy and his grandmother up in Moreton and Charlie said the bank started proceedings to foreclose three weeks after they missed a payment. This family has fallen on such hard times this year. Both parents were incinerated in that tragic traffic accident up outside of Mansfield and the family farm was left to the children. It has largely been paid off but not quite and the kids have been trying to set up a business to keep themselves afloat so they can maintain and pay off the property and that way all stay together. Paying for their parents' funerals and getting lawyers in a bid to keep the farm took all the money they had and the bank hasn't been that lenient it seems. And after this valiant effort to save this livestock, they have been given only a couple of months to vacate the property. Not enough time to achieve their plan of taming these beautiful, beautiful horses to saddle."

They remained silent as the second truck pulled up. A lot of lowing, the thunder of feet as Josh opened the gate and Coskins' cattle clattered down into the yard then were sent down another raceway to another lakeside paddock for grazing, settling and watering, clearing the yard for the next truck to off-load.

And on it went until the Hereford herd wandered calmly down the ramp and into the dirt arena, Bawldy tiredly leading the way. He immediately found a shady strip of ground at the side of the fence and lay down, almost instantly dozing in the last of the day's light. Clarrie wandered across to make sure he was unhurt. Singe marks and small burns marred his hide, but up on the mountain she'd been so sure he'd been shot she wanted to be sure an injury like that hadn't gone unnoticed. But he seemed just to be tired and sore and she patted his fluffy white head and left him to sleep a while.

The cameras kept rolling as Clarrie left the bull and strolled across to toss feed into the yard for him and the horses, taking the time to run her hands down the big grey's legs, checking for injuries from the hard ride down. Only when the stock was tended would she have time for anything else. Charlie watched her over the railing, noting how well she worked with his mother's horse. Then Chris and Josh appeared leading Titan,

Jasper and Jingo, having retrieved them from the brumby herd.

In the approaching dusk they continued to tend the stock, Clarrie occasionally glancing at the sky and the huge grey plume that blackened the mountains to the east. For the first time she noticed the small blisters on her skin and felt the soreness of exertion in her legs and back; she realised that some of her hair was singed, that her face felt hot and scorched, and her eyes burned – were still burning. Then tears rose to wet them, the world around her blurring fully as she surveyed the yards and the cows and the horses, her brothers and little Shy carting buckets of water to wet scorched coats and wash clean any cuts the horses had sustained. They had made it down the mountain, she realised, not completely unscathed but none had died. None had been lost to the flames. And with that she folded up and plopped down in a heap in the dirt and sobbed uncontrollably into her hands.

Josh reached her first; pulled her back to her feet and let her shed her grief for her parents and the elation of their survival on his shoulder, Clarrie muttering and sobbing inconsolably, "Nothing burned. Nothing burned."

They stood for long moments, Josh's arms protectively encasing her until a grey Four Wheel Drive pulled into the yard area, the local vet and his offsider alighting and wandering to the yards.

"Oh no, we simply can't afford this," Clarrie muttered, her head shaking with the acknowledgment that she simply couldn't cope with any more. She eased herself away from Josh, who rolled his eyes skyward and followed her to the yard fence.

"Hello, Stewart, what can I do for you?" Clarrie asked bluntly, immediately noting the stethoscope around his neck and his black instrument bag hanging from his assistant's hand.

They already owed him money.

"I've come to check the stock for you ..."

Clarrie shook her head. Another vet bill now would certainly lose any chance of them trying to catch up the back payment to the bank before the foreclosure took place; it would negate any chance of them overturning the bank's decision.

"This stock needs checking, Clarrie. After what you've all been through there is no doubt in my mind that many will be suffering smoke inhalation. They need checking and the affected ones separated for regular monitoring."

Clarrie's arms fell to her side and her breath left her. She knew he was right. She knew how restricted her own lungs felt, of course the stock needed attention. So that would be the end of it. After all they had been through they would still lose Spur-Lea, to vet bills. Her shoulders slumped as she sadly accepted defeat, as her heart started breaking. She felt Josh's arm close around her shoulders; he was still there supporting her, and she sighed, and fought back tears that all this had been for nothing.

"No charge on this, Clarrie," the vet assured her. "With what you kids did up there today there's no charge on any visit or treatment any of this stock needs. It's on the house, and I take my battered hat off to you." And indeed, he lifted his dusty Akubra then dropped it back on his head, and said to his assistant, "We'd better check on that Hereford bull over there first."

By now, Charlie had wandered closer and heard the conversation; he noted Josh's arm around his sister's shoulders, noted her tear streaked face, and looked worried.

"She's okay," Josh assured him and let his arm drop away, "but I'll keep checking on her."

"That's okay," Charlie replied, his hand gripping Josh's shoulder, "and I'll keep checking on you. Come on, let's get up to the house and tend to ourselves before Stewart needs us to separate the stock."

And together they wended their way through the yards to the house.

❧

CHAPTER SEVENTEEN

Mid-morning the following day, Clarrie and Charlie followed the vet around the paddocks taking note of individual animals he considered needed watching. While all beasts showed some degree of soreness or fatigue, only about a dozen showed some level of breathing difficulties and required closer monitoring. "They might just need a period of quiet rest," Stewart said. "We'll know in a week or so which ones have suffered long term damage."

Charlie looked up as an unfamiliar car swept up the road towards Spur-Lea. When it turned into the driveway and headed towards the house he excused himself and strode off to deal with the uninvited visitor. Clarrie continued to follow the vet and felt pleased she could relate to Nanna Kate, through Chris or Charlie, that Bawldy was fine and just required some time to restore his energy. She and Nanna had still not spoken much, only short replies so they could manage the house and Shy-Lee in reasonable harmony. With Nanna Kate taking over the care of Shy-Lee, she was free to escape the house and stay in seclusion and thereby avoid the critical eye of her Gran, but it hurt knowing their closeness would never be rekindled. She left Bawldy in the yards so Nanna Kate could visit him and assure herself that the last love of her life was indeed safe. She gave Bawldy a big cuddle and wandered down to the paddock to check again on Jasper, noting as she wandered down the raceway that Josh was already down tending to Jesse. She was pleased he was staying on for a few days while he organised somewhere to stay and somewhere to keep Jesse. Right then they needed all the help they could get, especially while they tried to find themselves somewhere else to live.

She grimaced that wherever they went it would be further away from the high plains they loved so much because the fire was still burning, tumbling down the other side of the mountain leaving devastation in its wake. There would be nothing left by the time it was done, and she wondered if Nanna was right – if more cattle had grazed the high country plains like they had for decades, would it have been this bad?

She sighed and joined Josh amongst the horses.

Back at the house, Alleena Lang swung her shapely legs out of the sleek sedan and stretched the tightness that still plagued her muscles. Charlie noted immediately the polished elastic sided boots, the trim cream moleskins, newly bought, and how pretty she looked now her face had been washed and the tiny burns treated. Her blonde hair had been swept back into a neat pony tail, making her look every bit a born country girl, or would have if the clothes weren't so new.

"Hello, Charlie," she waved and smiled broadly, her greeting exuberant, which he considered was most appropriate seeing they had all survived.

Charlie smiled back just as broadly and nodded, surprised that he was glad she had come back to Spur-Lea. She had lingered the previous evening as the film crew had packed up; she had hung around the yards, seeming to want to chat but knowing they were all terribly busy with the stock. Eventually, he had turned around to talk but she had gone. He had felt disappointed at that, but didn't know why he should.

She locked her arms around his neck as soon as he reached

her, which took him back a bit. He couldn't remember the last time a girl had hugged him – if any ever had.

"Charlie, we have to talk," she said. "When I told you this thing would go global, you have no idea just how global it went last night."

Charlie shook his head. As far as he was concerned this whole 'thing' was over. They had all escaped the flames and now had to put their priorities in order. The first was beating the bank, but the phone call that morning hadn't given them any leeway even though he had begged. They had to find somewhere to live in a hurry, with no money, and paddocks full of livestock. They could sell Coskins' cattle but they weren't in a fit state to sell, and the paperwork changing over ownership still had to be done, if they could find old man Coskins ... so many things thwarted them being able to continue living their lifestyle.

"We've got other things we have to put our attention to now," he negated any further involvement in the news broadcasts. He just didn't have the time or the energy.

Allee clutched his hand and started walking towards the house. "Come on, this is for your benefit – we have to talk to Nanna."

Over the next few days, Clarrie avoided the house, taking to massaging Jasper for long hours and lungeing the stiffness off Cascade; anything other than staying up at the house where Nanna Kate now ruled the roost. She had reinstated order from the chaos that had overtaken them; she had gone through her daughter's belongings and bundled them up for donating to the poor, and her son-in-law's, letting the children first go through the piles to retrieve any keepsakes they wanted. Charlie snaffled his Dad's rodeo buckles and belts, Chris his Dad's Akubra hat, while Clarrie gathered all the photos of her mother and her father, and them with their children; it broke her heart to see them, but she did not ever want to lose those memories. She hoped one day she would forget what she had seen and caused.

In Clarrie's absence from the house, Alleena Lang's film crew came and went, Charlie's absence from the stock yards duly noted as he was kept close to Allee. Josh and Clarrie managed the stock, and she noted at times how their laughter sometimes rang out over the fields, and how the horses lifted their heads, even Flaming, who had settled in to life in captivity, albeit by a beautiful lake and in knee deep grasses that proved more luxurious that his treasured high plains. But where would they be in a few weeks time, she sighed. And where would Josh be?

&

CHAPTER EIGHTEEN

A week later, on one of the final interview days with Alleena Lang, with cameraman Lew and his support crew working his magic behind the cameras, a gold sports Mercedes swung into the property and pulled up at the house. Karl Bradley alighted from the vehicle, a briefcase in his hand.

They'd been having fun up until then, Allee asking impromptu personal questions, getting them all relaxed, getting them to ignore the cameras as they congregated on the front verandah. She'd already collared Nanna Kate and had her life story, revealing to the world on film that if there was anything in life Kate Norton was proud of it was being a direct descendant of the renowned drover 'Clancy … of the Overflow'.

"And how do you know your grandfather was *that* Clancy?" Allee had asked her, grinning.

A twinkle had touched Nanna Kate's eyes and she'd smiled subtly. "Because the family owned half the mountain before the government claimed it for a national park, and because we maintained the last Cattle Station in the high country and because we maintained the last pure bloodline of the initial Hereford stock imported to this country, the reason we were given the right to graze the plains for Bawldy and his girls, and because I have photos of my grandfather with Banjo Patterson on Overflow Station. That's how."

That concreted the facts Allee had revealed in her earlier filming, points that had gained public support and heightened the heroic feat the teenagers had accomplished. They were of 'Clancy' stock; they had his backbone.

"And why did you go on that horrendous ride, Chris?" she completely changed tack, catching Josh and Chris prodding each other off to one side.

Caught off guard, Chris simply replied: "She's my big sister and I just do as I'm told. She said 'saddle up and let's go,' so I did."

Clarrie scoffed. "You do not always do as you're told – where did that come from?"

The cameras kept rolling as Allee laughed. She flashed a glance at Charlie as she noticed the bank official stepping from the car, then she turned serious. "Okay, Nanna Kate, you have already told me about how the kids came up to save the horses from the cull and why their parents weren't with them, such a tragic story, and now this young family is being forced off their land only weeks after defaulting on a payment because things had become pretty tough. That's not very fair is it?"

By now the bank official had honed in on Charlie who had risen and segregated himself from the group – this was a private matter that he didn't want on camera. The man pulled an envelope from his satchel and began to pass it to Charlie.

The cameras swung that way and a hush fell over the verandah. This was it – the dreaded eviction notice. Yet Allee smiled broadly and worked her way closer. This was great news broadcasting – Big Bank Eradicates the Little Man. Only not this time. She could see the caption heading 'David beats Goliath', and moved closer.

"Charlie, don't take that!" she interrupted. "There have been some developments over the past few days, and the National News Service and I are happy to tell you that all the outstanding debts for Spur-Lea are going to be covered. You don't have to go anywhere. A public fund was started up by a member of the public after people found out you were losing your home. Enough money has poured in over the past 48 hours that Spur-Lea is paid for. You all own Spur-Lea."

Charlie's face fell, the news taking a moment to sink in. He wanted to ask if it was really true but just stood blank faced, slightly aware of the whooping and cheering going on on the verandah behind him. A glance at Clarrie and a tear rose to his eye, matching the tears rising in hers. They had both worked so hard; they had all gone without, life had been real tough, and now ... this. He heaved a deep sigh and just stared at the man with the envelope. Then he glanced at Alleena, who nodded that it was real.

"I'll make an appointment and come into the bank to settle up," he said, wanting to grin but not wanting to seem smug. But his smile was growing as he glanced back at Allee Lang. She was an absolute miracle, and a doggone angel to look at.

The man put the envelope away and grumpily headed back to his car, Allee calling after him. "Don't ever underestimate the power of television, and I can only imagine the damage this has done to your bank. Think twice before you pull this on anyone else who's down and out because I'm always looking for a good story."

The car reversed out, Charlie's grin growing wider and wider.

On Allee's signal the cameras stopped rolling. "As I just said," she said genuinely to all on the verandah, "television is a very powerful thing. We have had an offer come in from a television producer wanting to do a show on your breaking of the horses, Charlie. The show will cover the breaking in of selected horses and be a weekly episode right through to the sale of them and then a follow up of how they fare with the new owners. Your time will be handsomely compensated giving you the funds you'll need to survive and maintain Spur-Lea. Are you interested? Please say you are interested – we've already done some bartering to get you what this is really worth."

Charlie shrugged – it was all happening so fast.

"Of course, it will include the whole family and how a breaker's life pans out."

"Am I going to be on television?" Shy-Lee piped up from Clarrie's lap. "I want to be on television. I want to be on television, Charlie."

Tears brimmed in Clarrie's eyes. Life was turning back to magic. She felt Josh's hand squeeze her shoulder from behind.

"If Charlie says yes, then you'll all be on television," Allee agreed, signalling the cameras to start rolling again, "all except Clarrie."

Charlie's face hardened instantly and the tears dried in Clarrie's eyes.

"... because Clarrie won't be here. She's been awarded a sponsored scholarship to Mt Holbrook Equestrian College where she will train under Phillipe Montague, who has just been appointed as the new trainer to the Olympic junior pre-selection squad."

Clarrie's hands pressed to her cheeks as her tears spilled over. Behind her hands she shook her head, more tears pouring down to wet her fingertips. She lifted Shy and put her aside, rose and strode away from the house, still shaking her head.

Josh rose to follow her but Nanna Kate's hand caught his belt and plopped him back down. "This is my turn," she said and hobbled down the steps to follow Clarrie.

She reached her at the horse yards, Clarrie shedding more tears unfettered.

"So what's your beef now, girl?" she huffed. "You've got what you wanted, but I don't see these being tears of joy."

Clarrie turned to her. "I can't. I can't go off and leave here. I can't go off and leave Charlie to look after all this and Shy. I'm needed here."

"Josh has nowhere to go right now," Nanna Kate said, "so he might stay on here and help Charlie, if he's asked nicely, and I guess I'll stay on to look after the family."

"You don't have to do that, Nanna. This isn't your fault ..."

"And it's not your fault either," the old lady snapped. "Things happen, girl. Things happen and it changes your life, and our lives are changing. I'm going to stay here and look after Shy and Bawldy, and you are going to go to College and show those toffy-nosed showponies how it's done."

Clarrie heaved an incredulous breath as her Nanna's arms enfolded her, warm and loving again. She started to cry again. "I thought you hated me," she wept on her Nanna's shoulder.

The old lady eased her away. "Whatever made you think that, girl?"

"You wouldn't look at me ... not once since it happened."

"Oh, child. It's not because I hated you ... it's because you remind me so much of your mother. When I see you, I see her." Her arm went protectively around Clarrie's shoulder as she turned her back to the house. "Do you know your Mum wanted to go to that Equestrian school when she was your age?"

"No."

"That's why, for her, it was so important for you to go there when you asked, because I could never afford to let her go, and she was good enough to ride in the Olympic squad, girl; none of that fancy-pantsy stuff, mind, but she could jump a horse like a trooper – she was always good enough, you know that?"

Clarrie nodded.

"And so are you," Nanna Kate added. "Do you know that? You will take that great big horse of hers and your precious Jasper, and you will go and show the world what you are made of. Born and bred on the high plains, you will show them how it's done. You are every bit as good as your mother was, Clarrie-girl. And do you know what else?" She smiled. "... all those old timers up in them hills that really know said your mother rode just like Clancy ... and you ride just like your Mum. And I am so, so very proud of you."

She kissed Clarrie's crown and squeezed her shoulders gently, and gazed up at the blackened mountains where the fire was eating everything behind another hill. She would return to the high country one day when the grass grew high on the mountain again.

EPILOGUE

Six months from that day, the show 'Taming the Wild Ones' went to air and attracted a huge television audience, Josh and Charlie demonstrating the gentler sides of taming the beast and becoming television celebrities – not exactly what either intended, but it paid the bills.

Alleena Lang auditioned for and won the role of 'Taming the Wild Ones' host, and left brother Paul to conquer the world of news reporting. Her documentary 'Fire in the Heartland' – the story of Clarrie of the Overflow' – won two industry Awards that year after gaining six nominations in varied categories.

The show's opening contained the following poem someone had written and sent in to the producer; it was recited during the opening scenes of the show as wild horses and cattle galloped boldly down the mountain ahead of the Alpine Ranges fire-front.

Clarrie of the Overflow

A fire flared in the ranges
that posed a wealth of dangers
to the horses and the cattle
grazing on the high plains grass
To escape the flames they thundered
while the cattle barely lumbered
down a gully, dry and rocky,
a rugged mountain pass.

Towns were fiercely burning
and the mountain fully searing
as flames ate all the country
near and far and high and low
for the heat had left it jaded
where water once cascaded
There was nowhere left to flee it
except down the Overflow.

And behind the herds rode Clarrie
who wouldn't let them tarry
for the fire was close behind her
and the sky was turning black.
On a grey horse, huge and tetchy,
his backbone arched and pitchy
'tween hands and heels she held him
barely moving on his back

And she drove those cattle boldly
while the horses rushed on wildly
pushed by a chestnut stallion
down the rugged mountainside.
To catch this wild-eyed creature
was to her the greatest rapture
but so far all best endeavours
he had constantly defied.

As flames bore down upon her
and the embers flew around her
she sent her riders town-ward
to quell the pace anew
and the ground around them rumbled
as the herds collective thundered
with the townsfolk cheering soundly
as she drove the mob on through.

And she raced the fire relentless
to a showground largely fenceless
And herded all the creatures
to the trucks to get away
And she rode just like an old bloke
of the high plains through the black smoke
As the stallion used his swiftness
in a bid to get away.

But she rapped the stockhorse boldly
and cracked the stock whip soundly
as she slid the grey horse rearing
across that open space
and the stallion baulked and cowered,
his escape thoughts duly soured
as he turned and took the truck ramp
to a better, safer place.

Now this story has been spoken
of the wild ride she had taken
down the rough and rugged country
where most would fear to go;
how she bravely saved the cattle
and the brumbies in the battle
while the fire was roaring o'er her,
Clarrie of the Overflow.

*****

Charlie and Allee married twelve months after the devastating fires ravaged the Alpine National Park.

Nanna Kate's home was destroyed in the fire but rebuilt by Charlie and Josh using earnings from their role as the breakers in the Wild Ones.

Nanna Kate, Bawldy and his girls returned to the high country plains five years later, after Shy was accepted to Mt Holbrook Equestrian Boarding School.

Clarrie and Josh maintained a long-distance relationship that continues to flourish as she prepares Cascade and Jasper for the Three Day Eventing circuit as a reserve on the Olympic selection team.

Josh's mother still resides with her sister in Sale, while Klemm Dodson disappeared from public view after being revealed in the 'Fire in the Heartland' documentary attempting to thwart the rescue of the horses and Bawldy.

Flaming was never tamed but remains the foundation stallion of Spur-Lea Stud at beautiful Lake Nadine. Ed sometimes comes to visit him.

&

Other titles by this author:

Penny's Silver Dragon – (Young Readers)

Bitter Comes the Storm (Fiction Novel)

The Horse Keepers – (Fiction Novel)

Ride a Crock Horse (Poetry)

Of Bushmen and Brumbies (Poetry)

Writing Poetry - Simplified (Text-book)

We Are Different, You and I (Children's Picture Book)

ABOUT THE AUTHOR

Western Australian born author Helen Iles writes in all genres. Her love of wild horses and writing bush ballads stirred the idea for this novel, while her strong background in training horses and emergency service work provided much of the finer details of this adventure.

A Creative Writing tutor, Helen writes adult and children's fiction, textbooks and poetry and provides manuscript editing services. She conducts writing workshops between penning the chapters of her next exciting novel.